MAYHEM NO MORE

Carli Cano Mystery Series

Book 3

Maryse Laflamme

• • • ● ● • ● ● • •

DEDICATION

As always, to Paul-Henri and Alexanne, my constant north stars, and to Olivia, the fiercest girl of all

Contents

UNLOCK CARLI CANO'S EXCLUSIVE PREQUEL—ABSOLUTELY FREE!

Ever wondered why Carli ditched the Big Apple for the colorful streets of San Miguel and a fashion wonderland of her own making? The answer is juicier than you think!

Sign up for my VIP mailing list and get exclusive access to the **prequel that spills all the matcha tea** about it! This is one backstory you can only get here because it's NOT available elsewhere and never will be!

So, grab Your Free Prequel, *Stitched in Deceit*—Available Only to My Insider Tribe:

https://MaryseLaflamme.com

Who needs a decoder ring when you can have the key to Carli's past? See you on the inside!

CHAPTER 1

J ust when you think your life is now drama-free, somebody
drops dead at your feet.

• • • • ● • ● ● • •

I watched as my neighbor from the house behind mine, Ramon Gonzalez, walked toward me in El Jardin, San Miguel de
Allende's main square, his approach steady and assuming the
gait of a cat on neighborhood patrol.

I smiled wide at him. In return, he waved at me and grinned,
though I thought he looked a little peaked, as if he were a
painting that had started to lose its vibrant colors.

When he appeared, I'd been gazing across the square at La
Parroquia de San Miguel Arcangel—Parroquia for short—the
famous church whose pink wedding cake-like spires stood
tall and proud, beckoning worshippers and tourists from all
corners of the world, attracting them along with our beautiful
UNESCO preserved town.

It was where my long-awaited day would take place, and quiet joy filled my heart as I gazed at it. Its spires seemed to reach as high as our perpetual blue skies and on up to heaven. Its bells would ring, their peals resounding like the triumphant finish of a grand symphony, to commemorate our happiness just ten days from now!

Seeing Ramon Gonzalez was a coincidence. I hadn't come here to meet with him or his wife, who I'm sure must have been close by as they did most things together, their lives as intertwined as the roots of old trees.

I stood from the wrought iron park bench on which I'd been sitting to greet him. We shook hands, then both sat next to one another. I scrutinized him. He ... well, he seemed different. There. More distant, perhaps? But no, there was something else ...

"¿Todo bien, Ramon?" All well, I asked him. Was he ill?

"Sí, Carli, *sí, todo bien."* He took a deep breath as if experiencing difficulties getting the words out. *"¿Y usted?"* And you. His voice faltered, and I noticed him gripping a handkerchief.

He didn't look or sound so well, as if a vacuum cleaner had sucked most of the energy out of him. But it wouldn't have been polite for me to say, so I ignored it, the same as I might overlook a tiny stain on his shirt so as to not embarrass him.

He wiped his forehead with his handkerchief as meticulously as if his life depended on it.

"Estoy bien también. Gracias," I replied. I'm also well, thank you.

Not wanting to bring attention to his flushed cheeks and the sweat on his forehead, I told him I was waiting for Manuel, that we were going to dinner to discuss final plans related to our wedding. We chatted about it, but I noticed his continuing shortness of breath.

He went on talking as if everything were normal. Said that Aurelia, his wife, was about town, shopping, and they'd agreed to meet here to grab a quick meal before heading home for a movie night.

He wiped his face again, and I wondered if now was appropriate for me to say something.

While deciding, I told him Manuel and I planned a long, relaxed dinner to cover all the last-minute details for our big day and honeymoon to follow a month later. Neither of us could get away for long right after our nuptials, though we had booked three nights in the honeymoon suite of a charming winery and spa just outside San Miguel. The thought made my heart beat faster, like a drummer's rhythm growing more intense during a song's crescendo.

Because we were sitting next to one another, my eyes weren't on Ramon the whole time, so it's only later that I realized I most likely missed some signs.

I'd been about to ask him if Aurelia meant to visit Carli's Secret Closet, the women's upscale designer resale boutique I owned and cherished, when he suddenly leaned forward, clutching at his chest.

"Ramon!" I exclaimed.

I watched, horrified, as his face turned pale, ashen, and he gasped for breath. It was a chilling transformation, mirroring a robust tree collapsing under a desert's summer heat.

"Ramon!" I couldn't help but repeat.

He fell quickly, his body folding in half, like a book closing. I reached out to him, to try to keep him on the bench.

"*¿Qué está pasando, qué puedo hacer?*" I asked. What is going on. What can I do.

He became very heavy, and I couldn't hold him up despite my best efforts. A man nearby made a move to help, but it was too late.

Ramon slid to the ground. His eyes turned glassy like a lively pond freezing over in winter, and saliva gathered at the corners of his mouth.

There were gasps around us, and a woman screamed.

My heart slammed against my rib cage, fierce like the waves that battered the cliffs of La Quebrada in Acapulco during storms. My whole head filled with the sound of it, obliterating all other noises, like that of the many people near us exclaiming, and calling out for help.

The way he looked, everyone could see that something awful had just taken place. He was as pale and still as a statue, his eyes glassy, vacant ... his chest no longer rising and falling.

No way to deny it. Ramon Gonzalez was dead. Right at my feet.

CHAPTER 2

I'd only wanted to wait quietly for Manuel.

We'd agreed to meet here in El Jardin and decide together where to go for dinner. Anywhere but at his own restaurant, he'd said. He needed to get away, yearning to escape the gravitational pull of his work. And besides, he had in mind to try a new place one of his chef friends had opened on the roof of a small hotel just up Calle San Francisco.

The spectacular view was worth the uphill climb that left us breathless, just like a tough ascent to reach a mountain top with the benefits of not only a great *vista*, but with a sense of accomplishment.

Or one could take a taxi, of course, but we preferred to walk, hand in hand, fingers interlaced in a comfortable, familiar clasp.

Manuel's Eatery would soon have its own rooftop dining option, a hot trend in San Miguel's Centro. The laughter and conversations that would take place there would make it even more of a nightly hit than it already was, thanks to my fiancé's culinary wizardry.

His *mole* sauce was a foodie magnet. Twice a week, he cleared the kitchen to make it himself, seasoning it with secret ingredients, guarding the recipe like a dragon hoarding treasure. It was the one thing he never turned over to his sous-chefs.

But I couldn't think of that now. People surrounded Ramon, and me, asking questions, exclaiming distress over watching a man collapse right in front of them—how could they not?

Their voices came at me like a muffled cacophony of sound through my loud-beating heart, my anxiety climbing, climbing, climbing.

Before I could gather my wits, as if through a haze, like a mirage in the desert, Manuel appeared. "Carli? ¡*Qué pasó, mi querida*!" He wasted no time taking me into his arms, though released me again immediately, reaching into his pocket at the same time.

Next thing I knew, he was holding his cell phone and had dialed 911, all while kneeling by Ramon and feeling his neck for a pulse.

The whole time, his eyes swept over everything around us like a hawk scanning for prey, his cop habits of old kicking in, much like a retired soldier with no desire to return to the battlefield, yet able at a moment's notice to revert to his fighting instincts.

Otherwise, he chose to manage his restaurant only, not crime scenes as he used to do. And he wanted me to stick to designing clothes and running my shop. He'd been angry with me for getting involved in murder investigations in the past.

At the same time, I'd gathered my thoughts enough to pull my own phone from my bag (Louis Vuitton, you know, one of the smaller epi leather ones), hands shaking beyond my control. I called Antonio Cano, the police's *Sargento de Investigación*—the detective sergeant. And my third cousin. Manuel's too.

"Antonio?"

"Sí, Carli." He spoke leisurely, as if this were a social call. He must assume I had questions regarding my wedding, or more instructions for him as best man.

Instead, I was about to bring down his mood a notch. A deep sigh escaped me, heavy like the drop of an anchor.

"My neighbor, Ramon Gonzalez, the one from behind my house, with the garden, *sabes*? He's dead. I mean, he just dropped to the ground right next to me. He was ... well, he looks ..., well, he looks dead. In El Jardin, Antonio. Right here in the square."

CHAPTER 3

The next morning I woke with a start, my first thought for Ramon. Dead at my feet! Dap, my cat, who usually slept curled by my head, took off, letting out his most fervent annoyed meow. He hated me bolting in the mornings, and it always startled him.

"Sorry, Dapperoo," I called to him as he left the bedroom. "Mamá is sorry ..." Mostly, he was Dap, short for his name, Dapper, because of his white paws on an otherwise jet-black coat, which made me think of dapper gentlemen from the Roaring Twenties. He became Dapperoo when I felt guilty for having hurt him, or wanted to lure him out from one of his hiding spots.

He didn't come back, but he would. He forgave quickly. I went to the kitchen and mechanically performed my usual morning matcha tea routine.

La Parroquia's beautiful spires could be seen from my rooftop deck, the irresistible allure that had persuaded me to purchase this place. That, and the just ten-minute stroll to my shop through the vibrant center of the city's heartbeat. And just steps from the main square where Ramon had taken his last breath ... sigh ...

How would I feel getting married no more than one-hundred feet from where he'd collapsed, his body forever imprinting the cobbled pathway with a ghostly memory?

Tears came to my eyes, echoes of my sorrow. I said a silent blessing for him and his family.

But, I had a boutique to run, and a wedding to prepare for, so what could I do but go on with my day?

I set my electric kettle to heat water to the ideal 170 degrees for green tea. Yes, I owned a kettle that got temps just right for different teas and French-press coffee. How else was a girl supposed to make the perfect cup of matcha? And Jamaica Blue coffee for her favorite person in the world, the love of her life?

Once ready, I poured water over a medley of mushroom powders—reishi, chaga, lion's mane, and maitake—followed by matcha powder and a dash of cinnamon for good measure. Coconut oil, and raw local honey from my family's *hacienda* joined the mix in the beaker, their aromas filling the air, a comforting perfume to me. I then plunged in the stick blender, its whir as reassuring as a lullaby, and blended it all into my go-to morning brew. *¡Perfecto!*

All the while, the image of Ramon Gonzalez, his features contorted in pain, slithering to the ground right next to me, clutching at his heart, seemed unwilling to dislodge itself from my mind.

From my second story kitchen at the back of my house, I had a great visual of the backyard of the Gonzalez home. It reminded me of El Charco del Ingenio, the well-known botanical garden on the outskirts of town where local cacti thrived. The Gonzalezes' yard resembled it, except for a few colorful bushes, and fragrant pink bougainvillea that saddled our communal wall, draping down both sides of it. I'd always relished this view while waiting for the water to heat.

This morning? How could I look at the garden the now-dead man had spent so much time and love on? Well, the one he'd instructed the employees of his landscaping company to spend time on. Still, he and his wife, Aurelia, loved their yard; they'd said so often.

Poor Aurelia ... I felt certain of her devastation over Ramon's sudden death. Their bond had always been remarkably close, symbolized even by the serendipity of sharing the same last name, Gonzalez, before they had married—a unique twist of fate in a country where women traditionally kept their own name after marriage. She had once told me that this coincidence had always seemed to them like a sign of their destined closeness. She must feel as if she's lost a part of herself. My heart ached for her.

I prayed that her children were either already gathered around her, or would soon be. And I *had* to pay her a visit. This morning.

We still didn't know what had killed Ramon. I just hoped it wasn't nefarious doings. The uncertainty added a touch of frost to the vibe of the otherwise warm day.

I had no plans to get involved at all ...

Me jumping into another investigation would rattle everyone—Manuel would wear that disapproving frown, my parents would wear their disappointment on their faces, and Antonio, well, let's just say I couldn't afford to put him in a bad mood. He was Manuel's best man, after all.

On another note, I felt the miracle of our family breaking their rule of no marriage between cousins, even fourth cousins like Manuel and me, to allow us to marry.

To distract myself from looking out the window, I played with Dap who'd resurfaced with my promise of treats. His green eyes reflected the sunlight streaming in as he pawed at a loose sock I kept pushing closer to him with my foot, then pulling back.

I just couldn't help teasing him, and he enjoyed it, pouncing on it over and over.

Out of habit, my eyes traveled to the kitchen window, and, unfortunately, onward to my neighbors' house.

At that very moment, their sliding glass patio door slid open with an almost inaudible whisper. Out came a man, of good height, fit, dressed in khaki pants and a short-sleeved collared dress shirt in muted tones, what men wore to avoid attention, to blend in, like a functionary.

Except, that is, for the black balaclava that covered his entire head and face.

It jarred me, and my palms felt clammy, my brow sticky with perspiration, my heart pounding faster and faster as if getting ready for takeoff.

I jerked backward. In the process, I lost my balance, and stepped on my poor cat. While his yowl pierced the silence, I knocked over the beaker, which tumbled into the stainless-steel sink where it clattered. Loudly. At the same time, Dap hissed at me. Understandably shocked and angry, he made a beeline for his favorite spot under the couch.

Goosebumps spread across my arms and the back of my neck, each one a tiny soldier readying for an attack.

The man glanced up at my open window, no doubt because of all the noise.

I forced myself to breathe while my skin turned cold.

Could he see me, my silhouette frozen in place, back pressed to the cool granite of the kitchen island behind me?

Could he hear the frantic drumbeat of my heart? Hear the scream I swallowed, my hand trembling over my mouth? If so, it didn't stop him.

He strode across the patio—his movements determined and purposeful—toward the path that led down the side of the house and to the street.

As he reached it and turned right, he pulled the balaclava off over his head, but I only caught a glimpse of the back of his head, and that only for a split second before he disappeared. Even in my distress, I regretted that I hadn't seen his face.

Hands shaking like leaves in a violent storm, I picked up my phone from the counter, its cool surface slick against my sweaty palms, and dialed Antonio.

The police should handle this. It wasn't my place ...

Fear tightened its grip on me when I realized that the man had to know that someone had witnessed him leave the house.

And that he knew exactly from where that someone had been watching ...

CHAPTER 4

"*Bueno.*" Hello. The low bass of Antonio's voice filled my phone's earpiece, the weight of his obvious fatigue rippling through the single word.

"Antonio, it's me, Carli."

Silence. No doubt he wondered why I'd identify myself since he had me in his contacts, and we spoke all the time. But my whole being shook like the bougainvillea on my back fence on windy days, so I wasn't thinking clearly. Plus he'd answered as if he didn't know the caller.

"I just saw something." I managed to get out through my constricted throat.

"*¿Mande?*" What. His voice rang through the phone, as clear and resounding as a stone dropped into the deep, abandoned well at our family *hacienda*. I remembered how, as children, we'd tossed pebbles in through the boards covering its mouth, the sharp, echoing plunk of them hitting the surface of the water breaking the usual tranquility of the ranch, something we did despite our elders' repeated admonishments to not go near there. Could I throw this new problem down that well?

I ignored his tone and fatigue and asked. "Can you come to my house?"

"Why?" Now, his voice was as rough as sandpaper, annoyance scorching the edges.

"I just saw something." I said again, as if I'd lost my whole vocabulary, my heart pounding like the hooves of wild horses running in a herd far into the *campo*. Countryside.

"I know, you said. What did you see?" He sounded bored as well as tired.

"A man came out of the back door of the Gonzalez house. You know, Ramon Gonzalez. Who died. In the square." The words filled my mouth with an acrid taste.

As if he could have forgotten that my neighbor had died yesterday, in the most public place in our town.

"Okay. So?" He asked, sighing with impatience.

His reaction puzzled me until I realized he needed more information.

"He was wearing a full-face balaclava." My voice shivered as I saw the man in my mind, leaving the house with that thing on his head. Somewhere deep in my bones, I knew. Knew that something terrible had happened.

"*¿En serio?*" Really.

Now he sounded curious, his interest flaring like a struck match. I pictured him sitting up straighter.

"Yes. Really. I don't make up stuff like that." I retorted, irritation prickling my skin like a thousand sewing needles.

"I'm going to send a car over there and then head to your place after. I'm at a house in Colonia Santa Julia where we found ..." His voice trailed off, mystery filling the space between us. Then, he added, "Well never mind that. I need ten more minutes here and then I can go." I wondered what he had stopped himself from telling me.

"Okay, I'll wait for you. I'm calling Manuel."

My words dissolved into the silence of a dropped call. Hands shaking, I began the process of making tea all over again. The beaker, unbroken, a miracle of survival in the chaos of the sink, sat amidst a mess of all the mushroom powders and matcha that had dumped out of it when it fell.

All the while, I kept calling Dap; I felt certain he wasn't all that hurt, but still, I *had* stepped on him even if only for a split second and with bare feet.

"Dapper! Dapperoo *mi amor*, treats, *mamá* has *treeaaats*."

I pulled four salmon treats out of a canister I kept on the island and placed them in his bowl, their scent, rich and tantalizing to him, floating through the room. He'd love that! He usually got two, at most.

Once the tea was ready, with still no Dap around, I took the first sip, long and deep, instead of, as usual, waiting until seated in my favorite chair on my rooftop overlooking not only the Parroquia, but a great portion of San Miguel, our *pueblo magico*—magic village—where Manuel, and I, and our families made our homes.

The *hacienda*, Hacienda del Cielo Azul, not ten miles from town, was where our ancestors had established themselves five generations ago, and where many descendants now lived. Many of us were involved in various local businesses. I let the strength of the memory of the land and the stone walls of the houses and buildings seep into me, grounding me in the rich tapestry of its history. The scent of my bittersweet tea reminded me that the annals of my family were filled with bitter and sweet times and that sweet moments always came around again.

My fingers danced on my phone screen as I finally cued up Manuel's number.

His deep voice filtered through, "*Hola mi amor.*" His tone had that familiar, infectious lilt that always permeated through me. Hello my love.

"*Hola, mi amor,*" my words echoed his, a smile involuntarily blooming on my lips despite the weight of worry that hung heavy in my heart.

There was a brief pause before I asked, "Manuel?"

His marriage proposal and my acceptance had been accompanied by a promise that we'd keep no secrets, especially where my safety was concerned, particularly when I got it into my head to solve a murder. I had a habit of attracting danger, you see, and he wanted to ensure that that would change.

My mind, of course, went to that night as it did so often.

On an early summer evening, the man I had loved forever had knelt before me and proposed. A soft breeze had teased my skin, mingling scent of the blooming flowers scattered between large pots along the edge of my rooftop deck, while distant music had reached us from the streets below.

His eyes sparkled, mirroring my own misty gaze. Hues of oranges and pinks painted the sky, casting a warm glow on his face, and surely on mine, all as if the Universe conspired to give our special moment the perfect background.

Magically, as the ring slipped to just the right spot on my finger, its weight foreign yet somehow perfect, a hush fell over our surroundings, the stillness inside the bubble we'd created around us soon broken by the melodious peals of the Parroquia bells, filling the air with a sense of joy. Each chime carried on the gentle breeze, weaving through the space between us, as if celebrating what we both wished had happened long before now.

Gently, I tugged Manuel to his feet. We stood close but not touching, letting time stretch. My heart continued its rhythmic symphony, its cadence reverberating through my entire being. My gaze went from the awe-inspiring diamond on my finger, my hand extended out like a fan, unsure it could move with this new shining object on it, and the captivating sight of my favorite person in the world—soon to be my husband. There he was, tall and strong in front of me like a fortress, promising to protect and love me for the rest of our lives ...

Feeling like I was clutching stardust, I let go and melted into his arms, his proximity sending a cascade of tingles along my skin. My head found its home on his chest, eager to become a permanent part of him.

As darkness had taken over, the bells had kept ringing, their notes full of hope for a future full of love.

Now, his voice coming through the phone line brought me back to the drama at hand.

"Carli? *¿Qué está pasando?*" What's happening.

"Well," I stammered, gathering my courage. "I was standing in the kitchen making tea, and I noticed a man sneaking out the back door of the Gonzalez house."

He said nothing, but a definite tension that hadn't been there before came across. I continued.

"Manuel, the man wore a balaclava ... he, well, I'm sure he heard me. I mean, he heard noise because I stepped on Dap, and the beaker fell into the sink, and ..."

He interrupted me. "I'm coming over, right now. Stay there!" he said, and hung up.

CHAPTER 5

Why was this happening now? Why? Manuel would fear I'd want to find out who that man was, what he'd been doing there—just like I'd done in the past when murders had needed solving. But I'd made a promise to him, and I intended to keep it.

I gave myself a strong reminder that this was Antonio's business to take care of, not mine. Yet ...

That man knew where the person who saw him lived.

I shook the thought away. Solving murders was behind me.

Soon, the soothing rumble of Dap's purr broke the tense silence. There he was, emerging at last—my silver lining amidst this chaos. I followed him with my eyes.

"Looks like we can't do anymore detective work now, Dapperoo ..."

He darted towards the treats, crunching one down quickly, and picking up another to carry upstairs as was his habit, his eyes darting confusedly at the remaining two. He wasn't accustomed to such a feast.

Since he was headed to the staircase, I decided that, yes, we should go to the roof as usual, even for just a moment or two. I picked up my teacup, and we went up, me apologizing all the way.

"Lo siento, Dapperoo, so sorry, my love."

In another break from routine, I lifted my eyes to the church's pink spires piercing the cerulean sky as soon as I stepped out onto the rooftop. The symphony of city life and traffic thrummed a comforting backdrop to the view and to my thoughts.

Manuel and I had chosen this house, my house, as our future home, rather than his. The view was to die for, and though we'd need to adjust if children came along, it was perfect for us for now.

When I'd first bought it, I'd revamped a smaller bedroom next to mine into a chic closet sanctuary with the help of a cousin. Bright lights from above and along the baseboards made every outfit pop. A magnificent triple mirror held court in a corner. A custom console sat center stage, its first row of drawers featuring neat compartments for my jewelry—costume, but hey, a girl could imagine storing diamonds in there *si*? Of course, she could.

Last week, I'd removed quite a few of my things from this dream of a closet to make room for my future husband's clothes, but I had access to a whole shop full of clothes, and making space for *mi amor* was a delight, not a chore. My heart swelled over the thought of all his things hanging next to mine.

A fair exchange. Less closet space, more Manuel.

I gulped the matcha rather than drinking it leisurely, knowing my doorbell was likely to ring any minute. Just as I took the last sip, I heard it through a speaker I'd had installed up here for that purpose.

Sighing, and reaching down to pet Dap—who'd forgiven me enough to lay sprawled next to my chair—I rose and went down the two flights to my front door.

The moment my fingers grazed the door handle, the assertive ring of the doorbell punctured the silence once more.

"Voy!" My voice echoed in the stairwell. I'm coming.

Peering through the peephole, I glimpsed Antonio, and another detective, his face etched in my memory from a murder investigation not even a year ago. Their stern expressions were a grim mirror reflecting how overworked they were, and with the shadow of a possible "incident" at the Gonzalez house.

I let them in, and we navigated upstairs to my kitchen, the sound of their shoes resonating on the stairs, and the banter from their two-way radio, static-infused words, zapping the air. They both turned down their volume.

"I hope you're not getting yourself in trouble again, Carli," said Antonio.

Rolling my eyes, which he couldn't see since he was behind me on the staircase, I retorted. "You say that like I only talk to you when there's trouble. And remember. This is not *my* trouble, but possibly the neighbor's."

"No, but you too often stick your nose into some trouble that is not yours ..."

We arrived on the second-floor landing, and I turned around to give him my best dirty look. He had the nerve to chuckle.

Once in the kitchen, we could hear men talking to one another in my neighbors' garden. I saw that the sliding door into their house was wide open.

I began recounting what I'd witnessed again, my words spilling out, unsteady, broken.

Our conversation was severed by the shout of a cop calling to another standing like a stone statue on the patio, except for his eyes that scanned everything in the garden. An urgent command to enter the house.

They'd found something.

He gazed up at my window, spotted me and nodded in greeting. He couldn't see Antonio and his colleague who were on the far side of the kitchen island. He quickly entered the house.

I turned around when the other detective spoke to Antonio.

"*¿Quieres que vaya allí?*" His voice vibrated with anticipation. You want me to go over there.

Antonio's eyes flicked to the window, and he came to join me to look out.

"*Si, vengo justo después de ti,*" he replied. I'm coming right after you.

At that exact moment, a jovial "*Hola*" echoed through the space as Manuel appeared from the lower level, announcing his arrival with the ease of someone familiar with my house—as he should be since he'd be living here in just a few days! My insides melted at the thought, but this was no time to indulge in such thinking.

The men's hands met in swift handshakes, the other detective departing with the urgency of a predator on the chase.

"Manuel, funny to see you here. You miss your cop days, huh?" Said Antonio, his eyes twinkling a little.

Manuel's retort was wordless—a speculative frown that pulled his brows into a tight knot and his mouth into a grim line, his go-to don't-mess-with-me look. His eyes were lasers cutting through our friend's joviality.

His silent defiance was cut short by the sudden crackle of Antonio's radio. An urgent voice cut through the static, the room going silent as if the air itself was holding its breath. The detective sergeant was needed at the Gonzalez house *pronto*.

They'd found a body!

Instantly, Antonio transformed. Gone was the laid-back friend, the detective humoring his cousin "just in case" what she'd seen turned out to be important. In his place stood a razor-sharp detective, brimming with intensity. A quick nod in our direction and he charged down the stairs and burst through the door, each step urgent.

An involuntary squeal ripped from my throat as I slapped a hand over my mouth.

"Cariño..." Manuel said, sliding his arms around my shoulders, a comforting weight that held me together. My heart drummed a frantic rhythm against my ribs as I buried myself in his embrace.

A chilling realization descended on me. The man I'd seen leaving the Gonzalez home, face shrouded with a balaclava, was most likely a killer.

He knew I saw him because of the commotion in my kitchen just as he'd stepped out that door.

And he knew I'd called the police.

Because, without such a call, a body in a house where only one person lived at the moment would never have been discovered so quickly.

My blood ran cold.

CHAPTER 6

T he next morning, I woke just as the sun was painting the sky in hues of golden light. Sleepy and feeling unsettled, I grabbed the Chanel silk watercolor caftan dress that I'd taken to wearing as a robe lately from the foot of my bed and slipped into it.

Dapper jumped to the floor and meowed softly.'

"Yes, another day, my little Dapperoo," I murmured.

I made my way to the kitchen for that oh so loved first cup of matcha tea. As I put all the ingredients in the beaker, Dap twirled himself round and round my legs, and my insides twisted, too, as I recalled what had happened yesterday just beyond my backyard wall.

Usually, I opened the kitchen window to allow in smells, the song of birds, and the sounds of the city beyond into my sanctuary, unless it was cold, or raining, but today, wasn't it best to leave it closed to separate myself from the past two days' events?

Since I had bought my house two years ago, I'd enjoyed the view of the Gonzalezes' vibrant garden every morning. Now, I felt compelled to avoid it, and wondered when I'd ever be able to look at it without sadness again. Maybe Manuel and I should live in his house instead of mine? No. I liked it here and so did he, and our plan was set.

Even though when Antonio had left my house yesterday morning to go around to the Gonzalez home to see about the body found there, it had been Aurelia lying lifeless in her bed.

Antonio had so far remained tight-lipped about it, refusing to disclose any details.

"Antonio, you always have so much to say. Why so quiet now?" I mumbled to myself.

In his defense, this was an ongoing police investigation. And he usually didn't talk about those. It's only when they were all wrapped up and tied with a bow that he turned into a chatterbox, spilling all the juicy details.

So, if Aurelia had been murdered rather than having died of natural causes ... I shook my head.

No *if* about it. Of *course* she'd been killed.

Balaclava Man, remember? I reminded myself.

How could one not ponder if this same individual might have caused Ramon's demise as well? I had assumed it was a heart attack, but now, with this distressing development ...

Ramon Gonzalez. The owner of a flourishing landscaping company, he seemed an unlikely target for harm. Why would anyone want him dead? And Aurelia even less.

Antonio and the other detectives speculated that it might be a robbery gone wrong—he'd told me that much. Well, he'd shared with Manuel who'd told me.

Their children would have to look through everything to determine that. Manuel had said that it seemed as if nothing was missing, but of course it was possible that the killer had been looking for something specific and knew where to find it. Which would mean someone who knew the couple well, someone who didn't need to ransack the whole house to find what they were looking for.

Could it be that the Gonzalezes had owned something valuable that the killer thought would be easier to get to with Ramon gone? But then, why not just enter the house when Aurelia wasn't at home?

I dismissed that thought; not logical. Whoever had killed her wanted Aurelia dead for other reasons.

Poor Antonio. He bore the weight of giving the siblings the heart-wrenching news of the deaths of their parents, just a day apart. One, the likely victim of a heinous crime, and the other, succumbing, perhaps, to a fatal heart attack. But maybe also a victim.

Questions gnawed at me—what could have caused it? Was it a natural occurrence, or was there something nefarious behind it?

I pushed those thoughts aside. My focus shifted to Manuel, and our big day. The whirlwind of emotions surrounding the tragic events could not overshadow the love and joy that awaited us. And not to forget that I had my own business to run, and that this morning called for me to be at the shop.

Sofia, a talented art student at the Institute de Allende, who usually opened for the day, had an exam and would only arrive at work around noon.

That left me with performing that task today. It happened rarely these days because she took care of it most of the time, so I enjoyed the occasional days when circumstances called for me to do it.

Nowadays, I spent most of my time running the business rather than being consumed by the day-to-day operations. Still, being in the front of the store held a special place in my heart. I loved it when women jostled for the fitting rooms, competed in a friendly way for who would get to try on the one-of-a-kind pieces I carried, and when a line formed at the register. Those were my favorite moments.

I'd gotten up later than usual today, having had a difficult time falling asleep after yesterday morning's discovery and the chaos that followed. So, I skipped going to the roof.

Was my world about to be thrown into turmoil again?

A hint of foreboding tried to creep in, but I refused to let it consume me. So what if Balaclava Man had thoughts about doing something to the person who had seen him?

It was all mere speculation—just a *might*. Perhaps he hadn't given it a second thought. This was San Miguel, after all, a place brimming with diverse noises, particularly here in Centro. I brushed aside the unease and forced a smile onto my face.

Yet, in moments like these, when uncertainty clouded my judgment, I liked to consult with my bio-father.

I flopped onto my bed, opening the nightstand drawer to retrieve the photo of him that I kept there for these very occasions. He had passed away before I was born, but a deep connection to him still resonated within me.

I had a perfectly good alive father who'd adopted me, my mother's husband, but at times like this, I preferred to consult with my bio-father who was more open to my, well, let's call them my adventures in life. Could that be because I got to choose what he said back to me? Ha!

In any case, when it came to matters of importance, I always sought his perspective. Only Manuel was aware of this secret, as I didn't want to risk hurting my *papá*'s feelings.

"Daddy, what should I do?" I whispered. "What if that man tries to come for me? Do I leave it to Antonio?" I stared at the photo, hoping to gain wisdom from him.

No immediate answer came, but that was alright. Sometimes, his responses would come to me hours later when I least expected it.

Rising from the bed after placing his photo back into the drawer, I made my way to the closet.

As I was slipping a vibrant Yves St-Laurent shift dress over my head, its bold red and white color blocks, accentuated by smaller yellow and blue ones, each bordered with black, created a striking effect, a sound from deep inside my house caught my attention.

My heart beating faster, I strained to identify the source, unable to recall if I had heard this sound before. It seemed familiar, right? Or was it new?

I stiffened as I puzzled this out. The dress clung to my shoulders, but I knew it was anxiety causing me to feel clumsy. With a deep breath, I pulled the dress down until my head emerged through the neckline, my arms settling into the armholes.

Despite feeling quite anxious, I went on with my routine. Inverting my head, I grabbed the flat hairbrush I kept in the closet and used it to gather all my almost-waist-length straight black hair onto my crown and tied it with a plain hair tie. My signature style. It made my cheeks appear more lifted and made my very bright blue eyes, inherited from my father, appear larger.

The whole time, I strained my ears, listening to the house. Nothing. Still, something had caused that sound and after yesterday morning, caution was called for, *sí*?

Then, there it was again. The sound that had jolted my senses. My hand moved to my throat where my heart seemed to have taken refuge. I felt as if I were in a horror movie with an invisible foe after me in my own house.

Slowly, I tiptoed out of the closet and into my bedroom, bare feet making contact with the wood floor. My path led me to the bedroom door, where I stood still in the doorway, ears attuned to my surroundings, anxiety fueling my every step. My heart, like a jackhammer, fluctuated between intense vibrations and brief breaks, providing no solace at all.

In that moment, I noticed Dap, who had hopped off the bed to stand beside me upon my entrance to the bedroom. He ventured into the hallway heading toward the living room and staircase. He paused midway, turning his gaze to me and fixing it on my face as if wondering what craziness I was up to now. Why wasn't I following him, he seemed to say. I trusted him, so I too stepped into the hallway. And listened again.

The sound reverberated through the air, emanating from up-stairs—undeniable now.

I drew in a deep breath as if I couldn't get enough air. I held a hand over my heart, feeling as if it would gallop right out of my chest. It did nothing to calm me. Where had I left my phone? Where?

Carlota Maria Garcia Cano! I chided myself. You are a coura-geous woman, one who will soon have her blue belt in Jiu Jitsu, and you did that fast, too.

What with the mayhem that seemed to keep happening around me since I'd moved back to San Miguel to find peace, I had felt I'd needed to know how to protect myself.

But training and applying those skills in real-life situations, as I'd had to that time in my shop, were two very different things. Would I have to do it again? Right now?

The sound came again, scratching at the recesses of my mind, awakening a familiar sensation.

I turned my gaze towards the staircase leading up to the third floor and to the roof deck.

Then, the dominoes fell into place. The door to the roof. *That's* what I'd heard!

Had Balaclava Man come into my house? From the roof?

I slapped a hand over my heart again in an attempt to stop its pounding. Pounding so loud it filled my head and kept me from hearing properly.

Yet, Dap, instead of hiding, kept looking back at me, a question in his green eyes.

Are you losing your mind, Mamá? They seemed to ask.

After a long stretch, he plunked himself down on the wood floor, delicately grooming his right paw with a detached grace. No signs of fear in his movements. He didn't look bothered.

Based on that, I made my way to the staircase, grabbing my umbrella from its rack on the way. I could use it as a weapon. Then, still on bare feet, I climbed the stairs, taking one step, waiting, then taking another. I stopped when I heard the sound again.

A moment later, a jingle sliced through the silence, jolting me. The familiar melody of Manuel's ring tone—*La Vie en Rose*—filled the space, its notes originating from the kitchen. My heart fluttered in my chest, a tiny bird yearning for the comfort of his presence. But I had to find out what was happening.

Under the lingering serenade of Edith Piaf, I continued my cautious ascent to the third floor. From the small landing at the turn in the staircase, where the final ascent of ten steps lay between me and the door to the rooftop, a surreal sight greeted me.

There, like a solitary dancer, the door oscillated, back and forth, on its hinges. Its squeaky hinges ...

I held my breath, heart racing, then calmed myself with two deep breaths and by visualizing myself at the altar with Manuel. Once calm, I could examine the situation with more clarity.

It could mean nothing. It could mean the worst.

CHAPTER 7

M y heartbeat echoing in my ears, I stopped six steps from the top. Any farther, I thought, could mean crossing the line Manuel drew in our trust.

A chill ran up my spine at the prospect of him questioning our getting married if it looked as if I were involved in an investigation. Again.

Not that he would. Manuel loved me. But the man had made me promise. And if I broke my promise ...

I spun around, and rushed down to the kitchen, my bare feet slapping against the cool concrete stairs with a rhythm of urgency. I had to call him before any thoughts of investigating anything dug their claws into my mind.

Snatching my phone from the kitchen island, I auto dialed his number.

He picked up almost immediately. "Hola, *querida*." I could hear the smile he no doubt was wearing.

"Manuel ... I think ... I think I need you here," I said hurriedly.

"What's going on?" His voice had tensed.

"The door to the roof was wide open just now. I'm sure that I lock ..." He didn't let me finish.

"I'm on my way. Stay downstairs, I mean, well, yes, come down to the front door."

He arrived in no time at all. Together, we ascended the stairs. Manuel led the way, and he stopped me when we reached the second floor.

"Wait here, Carlita, *por favor*. Hold your phone ready to dial 911." He looked at me seriously. I opened my mouth to speak, but no words came, so I closed it.

He squeezed my hand and planted a quick peck on my cheek before continuing up the stairs. Once he reached the landing where the staircase took a right turn, I couldn't see him anymore. I heard his footsteps, then the roof door opening slowly, then closing, then ... nothing.

My heart slammed away in my chest, and I so wanted to join him. The image of him stepping onto the roof and potentially facing an intruder or even a killer—without the security of the gun he'd once carried as a detective—sent a surge of apprehension through me.

Finally, he appeared on the landing and looked down at me.

"No one up here," he said, scratching at his jaw.

I pondered this. "I wonder how ..."

He gazed at me, eyebrows furrowed, eyes dark with wonder and worry, as he interrupted me.

"Did you leave the door unlocked, Carlita?"

My first name was Carlota, but I never let anyone call me that. I didn't like sharing it with the tragic Princess Charlotte of Belgium, who became Carlota of Mexico after joining her husband, Archduke Maximilian of Austria, in a doomed French intervention here. Their failure led them back to Europe, where Carlota proceeded to lose her mind.

I loved my *mamá*, but who gives their daughter the name of a woman with such a history?

So at the age of twelve, I had adopted the name Carli, a deviation only challenged by my parents. When Manuel wanted to be serious, though, he called me "Carlita," and only he was allowed to do so. What genius that he'd figured out how to use my real name when he wanted, but without offending me!

I looked at him, annoyed at his suggestion that I might have neglected to lock the door. "No, I wouldn't do that. You know it!" Crossing my arms, I gave him that look that meant he had best not continue that line of questioning. Or any other.

His question shook me, but was it possible? Had I left the roof door unlocked? The thought sent a shiver down my spine, like a foretelling.

"Okay, well, let's go through the rest of the house," said Manuel.

I followed him without a word, feeling unsettled. We found that nothing had been disturbed or taken.

"That's so weird, right?" I asked, looking around my house, confused.

Manuel said nothing, just nodded slowly, looking deep in thought. Finally, he spoke. "If anyone was here, they're long gone." He reached for my hand. "Were the roof dogs barking when you heard the door?"

I thought for a minute. The dogs barked frequently enough that I didn't always notice. "I don't think so ... I don't know for sure. But Dap was calm. He wanted to go to the roof."

So, I had either left the door unlocked—and that kind of door wouldn't stay closed without being locked—or someone had picked the lock just to open the door, perhaps to send me a message ...

The thought of an unknown presence in my home while I slept sent a cold shiver through me, especially since Aurelia Gonzalez had been killed in her bed ...

CHAPTER 8

An hour later, Manuel left, and I traced my usual path to Calle Canal where my store was located, in the heart of the tourist area.

Before flinging the doors open to the public, the soothing rhythms of Latin World music would fill the air, accompanied by the sweet scent of candles (far from the clothes).

As I paced through the aisles, adjusting the clothes on hangers, I could hear the murmur of fabric against fabric, one of my favorite sounds. A sweep through the changing rooms confirmed nothing had been forgotten in there the day before.

This ritual was more than a routine, it was nourishment for my spirit. I reveled in the splendor of my queendom, a space carved out in my cherished hometown by my own hands.

The only cloud over my day? Ramon and Aurelia both dead ... one murdered, okay, *possibly* murdered, no, *definitely* murdered. And the other? No way to tell yet.

And of course, finding my rooftop terrace door opened and swinging on its hinges the day after I'd seen a full-face balaclava-clad man leaving the Gonzalez house.

My mind whirled and spun like a *piñata* pushed about at a child's birthday party. I shook my head. As a soon-to-be-bride, other things should be occupying my mind.

Not five minutes after unlocking the door to welcome customers, the windchime tinkled as the door hit it, announcing someone's arrival. I preferred the melodious chimes to the electronic bells too many stores had nowadays.

¿Y la personalidad, dónde está? I often wondered, when entering generic shops, one just like the other? What about personality.

A smile bloomed on my face when I raised my eyes and gazed at my best friend since childhood, radiant as the celestial body she'd named herself after, stepping over the threshold and into my world.

Luna! Born Leona Gabriella Aguilar de Leon Lopez, she'd renamed herself Luna at age seven, after reading a book about a girl with gumption named Luna, and had decided on the spot that she wanted some, too, oblivious to the spark of audacity she already showed by changing her name. We had the renaming of ourselves in common.

Years ago, we'd been sitting on the verandah of my parents' home on the hacienda one evening, sharing a glass of wine, and I'd asked her why she hadn't renamed herself Sunny to match her personality, instead. With a twinkle in her eye, she'd said no one could look at the sun for very long because it would burn their retinas. But people could keep their eyes on the moon for much longer, and it had more power. "I mean, the thing moves tides, *chica*!" She'd exclaimed.

Words weren't needed now as we sauntered toward each other, meeting halfway between the cash register and the front door to exchange a heartfelt hug. She encircled me with her arms, and I relished the warmth she exuded, and the faint smell of her signature scent.

"Hola, chica." She said in greeting, her gravelly voice enchanting me as it always did.

"Chica to you." I replied, giggling.

Today, she wore an embellished-waist gown with a pleated skirt. Once a ball gown, my head seamstress, Josefina, had altered it by letting out the waist a little and shortening it to just above Luna's knees.

Spectacular Christian Louboutin So Eleonor ankle boots graced her feet. The long-haired calfskin was fashioned into a Madagascar animal motif with beautiful tone-on-tone stitching and, of course, red soles. The whole ensemble ... worked. On *her*. Flair should be her middle name, I often said.

"So, tell me everything," she said, as she claimed a high stool by the triage counter, patting the seat of the one next to hers, inviting me to join her.

En route to the shop, I'd texted her to ask when she could talk, that I had a lot to share. She hadn't responded, hadn't called, yet here she was. A good *amiga*. Friend.

She'd heard about the tragic passing of Ramon and Aurelia Gonzalez and knew I would be upset.

"Well, you know ..." I said, taking a deep breath and shaking my head side to side.

"Ah, and just before your wedding, too."

"¡Lo sé!" I know.

"You want me to get us drinks at the cart?" She offered, nodding her head in the direction of the courtyard.

"Sure. I need to stay here. Sofia doesn't come in until noon today. Exam."

"Ah, *sí*. Okay, I'll be right back."

"Make sure they use oat milk for me!"

"Yes, yes, Miss Healthy. Of course."

She grinned at me and winked.

"Ha, ha."

Waving at me over her shoulder, she walked toward the door.

In no time at all, Luna came waltzing back in balancing two cups, and a miniature red shopping bag hanging from her arm, no doubt containing pastries. My mouth watered and my stomach growled, reminding me that I had not eaten yet due to the morning's events at my house.

She'd just deposited the coffee and pastry bag on the register counter, when suddenly, the door swung open, and a man poked his head through the doorway, hesitated, then queried, "*¿Hola, la* Señorita Cano?"

His eyes darted toward Luna before settling on me.

Luna and I glanced at one another then turned our heads back to the man.

"Sí, estoy aquí." I replied. I'm here. Holding my breath, I observed him intently, as if later I'd be quizzed on what he looked like.

But, despite having asked for me, he seemed taken aback to find that not only was I present, but addressing him. It didn't escape my attention that he was of the same body type as Balaclava Man.

As he was about to step into the store, two women approached from behind. Clearly uncomfortable with their presence, he paused, seemingly calculating his next move. In a display of awkward politeness, he held the door open for them. Once they had entered, he quickly closed it, choosing not to follow them inside.

The women, oblivious to the drama, began to browse the clothing racks, while Luna and I stared at the man as he scurried through the courtyard toward the street.

CHAPTER 9

L una and I finally turned to one another, and the two women, as if suddenly aware of our odd behavior, looked at us with questions in their eyes. I shrugged at Luna as if to emphasize to the women that this was nothing, but my heart slammed against my chest.

As if we'd agreed to this, we made our way to the triage counter and casually began to pick up and assess clothing that had been brought in by consigners, making a pretense of that being our only concern. If only.

If that had been Balaclava Man, how had he found me so fast?

Of course, once he knew who owned my house, something he could look up online at the Registro Público de la Propiedad Federal—the registry of property ownerships—he'd know my name. And he could then have found out about my shop, though I couldn't think of how, at least not so fast.

Could this be *cartel* business? They'd be able to find someone like me quickly. They probably had people in all government offices. All of me shook at the thought. I couldn't see the Gonzalez family involved in crime. Ramon worked—had worked—hard at his business.

His mild-mannered wife had volunteered with charities, sometimes helped her husband, consigned some of her clothing with me, spent time with her Música Clásica Esencial friends.

Their three children were all well-educated and in the medical field. Graciela lived in Albuquerque, New Mexico where she worked as a nurse. Leonora, also a nurse, lived in Guanajuato with her husband, Pablo, who owned several tourist shops, and their young son. Alejandro was a well-respected doctor who lived in Mexico City with his wife and two children.

No, I just couldn't see it.

And yet ... they were both dead. In less than twenty-four hours. These things didn't happen in real life except by design, or at the hands of criminals. *¿Sí?*

If a *cartel* was involved in the death of Ramon and Aurelia, what did that mean for me? The one who had seen Balaclava Man?

The violence of *cartels* had forced many people from their homes, even from Mexico, going north into the U.S. in order just to stay alive. Would that happen to me? Would I, would my family, be forced to leave everything we loved here because I saw a man walk out of the Gonzalez home?

I shook the thought away; ignored the palpitations of my heart. No such thing would happen. A less despicable explanation for the deaths would present itself, said my optimism working hard to tamp down my body's reaction to the visit.

My hands were shaking, which I realized when Luna put a hand over mine to still them.

"Chica, what's going on? Do you know who that man was?" She spoke in a low voice so the customers wouldn't hear.

"No sé, Luna, *no sé*." I don't know.

We continued to whisper while the women continued to browse, one of them entering a changing room, her arms laden with several garments.

The soundtrack began to play another song, everything in the shop seeming to be just as it should be. Except for that weird thing of the man poking his head in like that.

Luna put down the dress she'd been holding, took a sip of her coffee, eyes on me the whole time. For a minute, I pretended as if nothing was off while I scrutinized a blouse, but my mind wasn't on it.

Finally, I looked back at Luna who'd kept staring. She raised her eyebrows at me, mutely questioning me.

I placed the blouse in the Keep pile, and whispered. "Luna ... what do I do? Manuel doesn't want me to mess with all this, but I'm sure that man knows I saw someone come out of the Gonzalez house. Otherwise, the police wouldn't have found Aurelia that quick." I picked up a dress and examined it.

"Well, maybe he's right, *chica*." She covered my hands again, squeezing them a little this time.

Then, her demeanor shifted as if her next breath blew a wind through her mind and changed it.

"But, also, you can't let him run your life just because you're about to marry him, you know." She said, a gleam in her eye, her natural mischievousness and "forget the rules" attitude in opposition to her words about listening to Manuel.

I couldn't help but laugh at this, though I kept it low so those two ladies wouldn't hear us and get curious again.

The door chimed and we both jumped a little as we turned toward it.

Manuel!

"Mi amor, qué onda?" I asked, surprised to see him here at a time when he met with his sous-chefs and the servers to go over the day's menu, which changed often based on what foods were available from local farmers and ranchers.

Still, I felt relieved it as him instead of that man.

"Manuel! *¿Qué hay de nuevo?"* Asked Luna. What's new.

"All the women ganging up on me," he joke-lamented, shaking his head, as if disappointed in us, though he still smiled.

He took my hand in his and kissed my lips lightly, then turned to Luna and kissed both her cheeks.

The two women darted glances at the love of my life; couldn't blame them. I'd be doing the same if I were them. Manuel always attracted female attention. He fit the Mexican version of tall, dark, and handsome so well, he might as well be the poster child, I mean, poster man, for it.

"I just came to say hello to my fiancée, is that okay?" He said, a playful sparkle lighting up his eyes.

Of course, the real reason was that he was here to check on me. This bothered me, but also made me feel safe and loved.

These opposing feelings collided in my psyche, but no time to analyze that now.

Just then, that same man walked by my shop, heading toward the back of the courtyard, his head turned this way the whole time. My heart seized, and it took all my resolve to not say anything to Manuel who didn't see him because he stood with his back to the display window.

The last thing I wanted was for him to confront the man while I had two customers in my shop. The gossip! The speculations!

"It's all good, Manuel, *mi amor*. Thank you for dropping by." I squeezed his hand as he hadn't let go of mine yet.

"Luna, as always, you look fantastic. Not as fantastic as *my* girl, but fantastic enough." He looked at me, his eyes full of love. My face reddened and my heart warmed.

Luna, laughing, slapped him on his arm.

We exchanged a few more pleasantries, and when the shoppers came toward the register Manuel said his goodbyes and left.

"Ladies, did you find any treasures you can't live without?" I asked them.

"Oh, yes, ma'am," said the brunette.

She handed me a pair of beautiful Dior butter yellow trousers, silk, the kind worn by Katharine Hepburn.

"Love these pants, y'all, and they're getting harder to find. Glad you had a pair," she said, a smile in her voice, her hand resting on them after she placed them on the counter.

"Well, like I said, I wish I'd seen them first." Said her friend, elbowing her playfully.

Looking at me, she added, "And I'll take this little jewel, if y'all don't mind." The blonde smiled as she handed me a hand-painted silk scarf, new, from a local artist I'd just started to buy from.

"Well, I'm glad you both found something to make you smile." I said, beaming at them both.

The women left the shop happy, just the way I wanted all my customers to leave here.

Luna said she had a meeting, so we said our goodbyes before I could tell her about what had happened with my rooftop door.

My thoughts and feelings of happiness didn't last long, as, not five minutes later, the same man once again made a pass in front of my store, this time, accompanied by another man, a bit rougher looking.

They boldly stared at me through the storefront window, then turned around and went back out of the courtyard and to the sidewalk.

My heart, for the ... how many times this morning?, lodged itself in my throat.

I had to tell Manuel. And Antonio. *¿Sí?*

Maybe not ...

I'd tried to tell myself it had nothing to do with me. But, with my neighbors both dead, men coming to my place of business in a threatening manner? After I'd seen Balaclava Man, and after finding my rooftop door open?

Even though it meant going against the wishes of the love of my life, and Antonio, I'd have to get to the bottom of it, and *pronto*. Quickly.

Because I wanted to make it to the altar in eight days.

Not end up like Ramon and Aurelia Gonzalez.

I had no desire to keep things from Manuel, but also had no intention of starting our marriage by letting him baby me—what kind of message would that send him? And Antonio? Well, I always felt that he—as much as I respected and loved him—took a long time to figure things out.

He'd reach the same conclusions as me, but in much more time than my patience could handle, particularly with my own life in danger. And it now looked like it might be.

I'd have to deal with my promise to Manuel to not get involved later. He'd forgive me. I didn't want to think about the alternative.

CHAPTER 10

T he two men had just disappeared from view when Sofia came into the shop like a strong breeze, a huge smile on her face, looking self-satisfied.

"I'm sure I passed it, Carli! I'll have a great note on my exam." She put her handbag in a drawer below the register counter.

"Sofia, did you see those two men just now?" I asked her, nodding my head in the direction of the door and the courtyard.

The smile slipped off her face at me ignoring her good news and asking her a strange question instead.

"Oh, men?" She swiveled her head toward the door.

"Hmm, I did pass two men leaving the courtyard when I entered it. I assumed they'd gone to the coffee cart. Why?"

I shook my head, gazing at the door and beyond. Then, remembering that Sofia stood in front of me, that she was an innocent in all of this, I turned my thoughts to her.

"Lo siento, Sofia, *lo siento.*" So sorry. I had jumped on her with questions without first addressing the most important thing to her this morning.

"Congratulations on your exam. I am proud of you!" I gave her a hug.

She beamed at me. Then, in the way that only teenage girls can, the smile dropped from her face and her mood changed, her expression clouding over.

"It's so good and I'm so happy, but something happened with my uncle."

Now she looked distressed, the corners of her mouth turned down, and her brow furrowed.

"Oh. What happened?" I tensed.

"A body was found in his backyard. Just yesterday morning!"

I gawked, unable to keep my jaw from dropping.

"How? I mean, yes, I do mean it, how? And which uncle?"

"A gardener, apparently. *Tío* Eduardo." I'd met her *tío* at her birthday party the previous year.

"A gardener?" I asked.

My heart slammed against my ribs, acting like something was after it and it had to get out of my chest to save itself. How many times would this happen today?

She nodded yes at me.

"A gardener is dead?" I held my breath in anticipation of her response.

"Oh, no, I mean a gardener found a body." She wrung her hands nervously, her eyes darting around the shop as if the inanimate objects in it, like the clothing racks, had answers.

"The gardener, he was planting an orange tree because my aunt pestered my uncle so much about wanting one and finally, he decided to have it done, and now, well, now, it's terrible, Carli, it's just terrible." She took a deep, shuddering breath, clearly struggling to hold back tears.

I remained mute, my brain on Pause. What was it with all the dead bodies around me in my life again, I couldn't help but wonder.

"And now what will happen to my uncle? Do you think he'll go to prison?" Sofia bit her lower lip, while her gaze flickered towards the door as if half-expecting the police to walk in.

"Oh, and what about my aunt and cousins?" She asked, as if she'd just remembered them, crossing her arms.

She looked at me in the same way as when waiting on me for instructions about the shop. But how could I direct her actions regarding a body having been found in her uncle's garden?

I managed to get my brain going again.

"Sofia, are you alright? Do you want to go home? Maybe it's best if you don't work today?"

If she left, I'd have to stay here until Esme arrived in the afternoon. Should I leave, though? What if those men came back while Esme was here alone? I couldn't allow that.

Sofia shuffled from one foot to the other, rocking her head left to right a few times before answering me.

"No, I'm fine. I ... well, I think I want to go to my uncle's house but my *papá* is out of town and *Mamá* is at work and can't leave, and I don't want to go alone."

She barely breathed this girl when she talked.

The Gonzalezes were dead, and a gardener had found a body in the backyard of Sofia's uncle's house. This kept getting closer and closer to home.

"Sofia, where does your uncle live?"

"In Santa Julia, at the bottom, you know, near that art studio. He bought the house years and years ago and then renovated it a little more every year and now there's a beautiful garden and they keep adding trees and plants, and now ... well, now there's a body in there too, actually a skeleton, but no, I think the *policia* took it away now. I wonder if we can even get into the house. My birthday party is supposed to be there again this year. I was going to invite you, of course. But now ..." Her eyes on me, she looked near tears. She stood in front of a full-length mirror and rearranged her blouse and applied lipstick.

"Ah, not a *body*. A *skeleton*?" I asked, crossing my arms.

Her eyes widened, looking like she just realized what a big difference that was, and she blushed, giving me a sheepish look in the mirror.

"So, the studio. You mean the one for new artists?"

"*Sí.*"

Not too far from here, in that case.

Then it hit me. That must've been where Antonio was yesterday morning when I called him about Balaclava Man. He said something about being in Colonia Santa Julia but then cut himself off. Chances were high that he'd been at Sofia's uncle's house.

So. Was this uncle somehow linked to Ramon and Aurelia Gonzalez and Balaclava Man? Or to the dead body? Or rather, the skeleton? If it was a skeleton, it would have been there for many months, or many years.

And of course, Ramon owned—had owned—a landscaping business, one that planted lots of large trees, a specialty. Had Ramon's company been the one to send the gardener who'd found the skeleton?

I'd heard a rumor about Sofia's uncle. He was a director of an IT enterprise based in Mexico City and went there often. But when I'd met him, he'd told me that he also often worked from his home here. I believed him to be an honest man, working and looking after his family.

However, the rumor was that he might have a cousin involved in a *cartel*. Not that this should reflect on him, but could have something to do with a skeleton buried in his garden, *sí*?

In the end, how would all this affect me, the one who did nothing but look out her window as usual while making her tea?

How was I to know that Balaclava Man would interrupt my ritual? No one could blame me for wanting to get at the truth, and right away. Not even Antonio. Not even Manuel.

I dismissed these thoughts from my mind because Sofia wasn't to know all this. A skeleton found on an uncle's property was enough for a young woman to handle. She didn't need to know that somehow, her boss might be affected by it, too.

"Ah, *lo siento*, Sofia, that is too bad. Are you sure you're okay? And your *mamá* and *papá*? How are they taking it?"

She shrugged, again showing her young age of seventeen.

"They're okay. Just upset. We don't know yet who that was or why it was in my uncle's backyard. The *policia* wouldn't even say if it was a man or a woman."

"They probably don't know yet. Was ... was your uncle arrest-ed?"

"Yes, but he was let go this morning because, because ... I don't know. But he's not allowed to leave San Miguel and a police officer is watching his house. I know he's lonely with my aunt and cousins gone to Dallas to shop." She pouted and sat herself on one of the stools by the triage table.

"Carli, can you come to the house, his house, with me? Could we bring him *comida*? My *mamá* says she'll go after this meet-ing of hers that she says she waited months to get, and the people are from out of town so they came just to see her, so she can't leave right now." Her eyes pleaded with me.

Her monologue turned into background noise for me, while I instead wondered if this skeleton might have something to do with the death of Ramon and Aurelia.

Why would Antonio not call to tell me, to warn me, in case this was a danger to me? I mean what with those men parading by my shop, and the one who knew I'd seen him leave the Gonzalez house?

I felt anger rising in me, until I remembered that he didn't know about the men stalking me at my shop this morning.

If he and Manuel knew that those two *vatos* would figure out a way to keep me under lock and key until the whole thing was resolved.

Wait, what had Sofia just said? Go to her uncle's house?

A nugget of a thought formed in my mind. What might I learn there?

"Sorry, Sofia, I was thinking what clothes to get you to triage first. You want me to go to your uncle's house with you?"

She nodded enthusiastically.

"Well ... we'd have to close the shop," I ventured speculatively, as if this were something I did all the time during business hours. Which, I never.

She looked a bit guilty at that but nodded her head again, the expression on her face somber. Sofia not talking meant her feelings were too big to get any words out.

Her big brown eyes with their flecks of gold looked gargantuan now as they fixated on me. At the same time, she twisted a strand of her long hair, which she'd worn loose today, around her index finger, a habit of mine she'd started to imitate a while back.

"I'd need to make a few phone calls first," I said while thinking about it.

"Okay, I can wait, triage clothes while you do that, but I should turn the sign to Closed, *sí*? So no one comes in because what if they stay a long time and then we lose our chance to go?" She pouted.

She knew how to make it sound as if it was my idea to go over there, as if *she* were doing *me* a favor.

And maybe she was. I might find out something to protect myself from Balaclava Man, and from the men from this morning.

"Okay, just continue going through the clothes already on the table," I nodded in their direction, "while I go into my office to make the calls. We'll leave in about fifteen minutes."

She beamed at me, but before she could start to thank me and turn the sign to Closed, those same two men opened the door, and this time, made their way in.

CHAPTER 11

They came toward me, forced smiles on their faces, as if they hadn't walked back and forth in front of my shop multiple times, wearing sinister looks.

As if the one on the left hadn't stuck his head through the door and asked for me and then left without saying a thing, less than two hours ago.

"Buenos dias." I greeted them, crossing my arms, mentally preparing myself for a fight.

"Buenos dias." They responded at the same time. One wore a sports jacket. I recognized the bulge just below his left armpit for what it was; I'd seen Antonio look the same way more than once.

Except that, in Antonio's case, it was legal for him to carry a gun—but not for anyone else in Mexico. Guns were illegal for all civilians.

"¿En qué puedo ayudarles, caballeros?" I asked, heart in throat. Gentlemen, how can I help you.

"Quiero obtener un certificado de regalo para mi esposa, por favor." Said the one who'd stuck his head in the door earlier, and who carried the gun. I want to get a gift certificate for my wife, please.

Well, it seemed a strange request, but gangsters had girlfriends and wives too, and I tried to convince myself that he did have a wife, that he wasn't here to check me out closer, to figure out what I might know, what I might have seen. So, I went with it, not wanting to go in the direction of asking him questions about his behavior earlier.

He bought the certificate, and I wrote it out myself instead of asking Sofia to do it. I wanted to minimize her interaction with them. Mine, too, but I couldn't just ignore them.

They stood right there in front of me the whole time, silent, sending an ominous vibe that wafted over me like a bad breeze.

Sofia tried to make conversation with them, starting by saying that his wife was lucky to have such a generous husband, but neither man even looked at her, their eyes riveted on me instead, so she turned back to the clothing, blushing at being so rudely ignored.

It burned me inside to have them in my shop, MY shop, and threatening me in this way, and mistreating my Sofia without even saying a word.

The "husband" paid in cash, nodded at me as I handed him the envelope with the certificate, but said nothing, just kept staring at me, along with his *amigo*. Intimidation tactic.

It worked.

To a point.

They said *adios* and left the shop.

Sofia turned to me. "They were strange, these men, Carli. Don't you think?"

I kept my eye on the door while replying to Sofia.

"Somewhat, but you never know about people. I'm sure his wife will be happy.

"I'll go make my calls now and do what you can with those clothes. We'll leave in about fifteen minutes."

"Okay, Carli," she said, joy in her voice.

She turned back to the triage table, and I went to my office, pulling my cell phone from my pocket as I went.

I felt uncomfortable about that visit. Very uncomfortable. Surely these men had something to do with the death of Aurelia, perhaps even Ramon's?

Why else would they come around like this? What were they trying to find out from me? What did they think I knew?

I felt my heart pinch a little. I'd have to break my promise to Manuel. How else could I find out who had killed Aurelia and who now seemed to be coming after me?

What if Eduardo was somehow involved in all this? What with a skeleton found in his backyard at about the same time that both Ramon and Aurelia had died?

If I was going to get to the bottom of this, might as well do it now. It needed to all be over before I said my "I do." In eight days.

And Manuel could not know.

This part might be a bit complicated, but I could do it. He was busy with the restaurant most days and many evenings. He wasn't the sort of fiancé who needed to know where I was every minute. Usually.

Forget returning phone calls now. My mind just wasn't on it. I left my office and locked its door.

"Sofia, I changed my mind, come on, let's go now. What do you say? And let's pick up coffees and tea and some pastries from the coffee cart. If we decide to have *comida* there, we can order something."

"Gracias, Carli!" Said Sofia, her enthusiasm back in full force despite her worry about her uncle.

CHAPTER 12

We could have walked to Eduardo Caldera's house, but with coffee, tea, and a couple bags of pastries, we decided to take an Uber. The driver soon arrived and in less than ten minutes we were out of Centro and in Santa Julia at Sofia's uncle's house. A yellow plastic police ribbon lay on the ground, attached to only one side of the door. No police officers around at all.

Eduardo came out of the front door as soon as the Uber stopped. Considering he'd spent a night in jail, he looked good for a man in his mid-fifties. He wore his thick curly hair cropped short, his mustache trimmed neatly, and most likely worked out—he looked strong. Strong enough to kill a man, perhaps? I shook the thought away. Even the police didn't think that right now.

"Sofia!" He called out and hugged his niece.

"Tío!" She exclaimed, hugging him back.

During their exchange, the Uber driver had taken off, careening away along the cobblestone street.

When uncle and niece pulled apart, Sofia put her hand on my shoulder and re-introduced me to him.

"*Tío*, you remember Carli Cano, my *jefa* from the clothing store?" Boss.

"Of course, I remember la Señorita Cano, Sofia!" He said, offering me his hand, his face cracked open wide in a smile. I couldn't miss the worry in his eyes, though.

"Señor Caldero, *hola*, it's nice to see you again." I replied, shaking his hand.

"Ah, please call me Eduardo. I consider you a friend."

"And please call me Carli," I replied, a part of me wanting to return his warmth on an equal level, but I found it difficult, what with a dead body, I mean, skeleton, in his backyard.

He and Sofia continued with pleasantries as he led us into his house. We entered a spacious living room, where the fourth wall, all glass, revealed the backyard and the now notorious garden. It was a deep yard, but the large hole that had been dug on the left of it near the back wall was visible, even from where we stood just inside the front door. A beautiful garden under the sun—a skeleton festering underneath it.

"Here, *Tío*, coffee for you. And ... I need a platter for all these pastries. Carli bought out the coffee cart," she said, glancing my way, a smile in her voice and on her face.

"You know where your *tía* hides them, go get one." He said, adjusting the glasses perched on his nose, and then heading to the sitting area closest to the back sliding door, offering me a chair facing the garden. He took a seat on the couch facing the chair, so he couldn't see the yard. Maybe he found it difficult to look back there.

"Eduardo, Sofia told me what happened. I just want to say I'm sorry you are going through that." I rearranged myself in my chair, and took a sip of tea.

"Gracias." He said with a sad smile, his face showing stress. Not surprising, of course.

"Here we go, my favorite people!" Said Sofia as she placed the platter of all those pastries on the table. Looking at it, I realized I'd overbought, most likely out of a reaction to this whole situation. A murder, maybe two, to figure out. Well, I corrected myself, for Antonio to solve, but how could I stay out of it as Manuel would want me to when my own life might be in danger?

Eduardo took me out of my reverie. "Carli, thank you for bringing Sofia. She's the sensitive one in our family, our artist." He looked at her with pride, and smiled while adding, "The one who worries about all of us."

Somehow, he put me a bit on edge. I felt there was something, or many somethings, being left unsaid.

Sofia swallowed a bit of pastry before speaking up. "*Tío*, do the *policia* know who it was yet?"

We all knew what she meant.

"Well, no, but Sofia, it happened many years ago, and it was ..."

His face flushed, the flush of someone realizing he'd said something he didn't mean to say.

Ah ...

The police either didn't know or hadn't told him yet who they'd found. Could it be that he already knew who had been lying there in his garden, and for how long?

As if he had the same thought at the same time, he leaned forward to pick up a pastry but knocked over his cup of coffee in the process.

Was it deliberate? It didn't seem so by the way he reacted, but maybe.

We all jumped up because the liquid quickly made its way across the coffee table in rivulets of pale brown, coffee and milk blended. I lifted the two things closest to my side of the table, a vase with gardenias in it, which scented the air beautifully, and a newspaper. Sofia took the platter, placed it on a side chair and speed walked to the kitchen, returning in seconds with a cloth to wipe up the mess.

"It's okay, *Tío*, don't you worry. You're upset, I know, it's not your fault. I'm cleaning it up. See?" She grabbed her long hair and wrapped it around a scrunchy she'd been wearing on her wrist, then leaned down, wiping the table in large circles, putting extra effort into it to show him it was getting done. "And then we can have coffee again. I give you mine, or I can make you some fresh, and you can have a delicious pastry."

"Ah, *gracias*, *mi* Sofia, *gracias*."

Eduardo made more noises of apologies, grabbing two books from the coffee table before the liquid could reach them. He also grabbed a set of keys that had been next to the platter.

Sofia, who seemed to not recall at all what Eduardo might have been about to say, whisked the soaked cloth to the kitchen, returning with paper towels.

I took them from the rattled girl's hands and wiped down the coffee table with them, dabbing at the coffee, getting as much of it as possible, then carried the drenched towels to the kitchen.

I opened the trash can to throw them in, but something stopped me. Right there, in full view at the top, sat what looked like several pages from a journal, torn into pieces, some very small, some a bit larger.

My heart lurched with surprise. A gut feeling told me that something in those pages would answer the mystery question of who had been dug up from the garden, just fifty feet away from me.

Still, I felt uncertain because would Eduardo leave evidence that could lead to himself like this in his own trash can? With police around? Either he was totally bemused about the whole thing, or there is nothing in those papers, or Eduardo had done it and wanted to be caught.

Without overthinking it, I gathered all the fragments and shoved them into my pockets, before dumping the paper towels into the trash.

I followed Sofia and Eduardo's voices back into the living room, but before I could sit myself down, and before any of us could take a sip of our drinks, or bite into a pastry, the doorbell rang.

We all startled, but Eduardo more so than Sofia and me.

"You expecting someone, *Tío*? When's *Tía* coming back, by the way? Now that this happened, won't she come back sooner?"

She asked the questions as her uncle walked toward the door. He looked through the peephole, and seemed to be using that as an excuse to ignore Sofia and her questions.

Instead, he opened the door.

And there stood Antonio and another detective, both frowning, in full detectives-on-a-mission mode.

CHAPTER 13

My heart sank. Fear gripped me by the throat. For sure he'd want to know what was on those pages, too. But, finders, keepers, *sí*?

Antonio entered first and stood in the doorway for a moment, staring at me, judgment in his eyes. I had already turned around in my chair to see who had come through the door. His look alone made me jump to my feet and return his stare.

"Antonio, *hola*!" Hello. My hands, of their own volition, clasped together in front of me, while I held my breath waiting for his reaction to seeing me here. Where I didn't belong. Where a skeleton had been found. Where one of his investigations was taking place ...

"Carli?" He looked dumbfounded. I watched as suspicion filled his eyes.

"I came with Sofia. Eduardo Caldera is her uncle." I spoke before he could think I was inserting myself into his investigation of the skeleton. Or the other thing, the Gonzalezes' deaths.

All the while, those pieces of paper burned a hole in the pants pockets of my Pierre Cardin set. It was a good thing the top, somewhat loose, reached halfway between my hips and knees and hid the bulk of the paper. It wouldn't rustle because the fragments felt a bit damp. Most likely I could leave here and take them home without Sofia or Eduardo knowing. And Antonio.

"Ah ... *veo*." Said Antonio. I see.

Nonetheless, the air thickened with his suspicions. And with my guilt, though I hadn't done anything to affect any investigation of his. Yet. Well, the pieces of paper ...

"Buenos dias, Señor Cano." This from Sofia, her voice floating in the air like soap bubbles at a child's birthday party, which released some of the tension.

"Sofia," he said, nodding at her in acknowledgement, a small imperceptible smile on his lips.

The other detective said not a word. He stood, impassive, his eyes trained on the windows and glass doors and on the garden beyond, presumably waiting for orders from his boss. Antonio did not introduce him.

"Señor Caldera, can we speak alone, *por favor*?" He said instead.

Looking rather nervous, Eduardo ran a hand through his thick hair before finally replying.

"Ah, *sí*, this way, to my office."

After they left, Sofia and I turned to one another. She shrugged as if to say she didn't know what that was about, and I shrugged back because I sure didn't know either, though I would have loved to insert myself into their conversation.

Sofia made to sit on the couch and get to that coffee and pastries, which I wanted to do also.

But loud voices from the office changed both of our minds, and we just stood, our eyes riveted in the direction of the hall down which Eduardo's office was located.

I'd noticed that the house's doors were thick, those old-fashioned ones built at least half a century ago, like the ones at my family's *hacienda*, and the plaster walls were also very thick, so for the voices to reach us, they had to be close to yelling at each other since the office was several doors down the hallway.

I placed a finger vertically over my lips, signaling Sofia to be quiet as if it were a game. Then, I took my shoes off and tiptoed down the hallway to try and hear what they were saying.

Sofia, her eyes large and bright, nevertheless felt compelled to say something.

"Carli!" she whispered-yelled, slapping her hand over her mouth. I turned around and gave her the evil eye. Her eyes grew even bigger, but she said nothing more.

I remained at least three feet from the door, but I could make out some words now.

"Señor Caldera, it's *muy importante* that you tell us all that you know. Your behavior says that you're hiding something from us, *sí?"*

I recognized Antonio's voice.

A muffled response. Eduardo, I thought. But what had he said? Why did he whisper?

"We've gotten information on a cousin of yours that went missing five years ago. What do you know about that?"

Another muffled response. Why was Eduardo's voice coming through like that when I could hear what Antonio said just fine?

"We'll know what really happened in time. Things will go better for you if you tell us what you know now, instead of after we find out for ourselves. I don't want to have to take you back to jail."

The doorknob rattled some, and I guessed that one of them had their hand on it. I tiptoed my way back to the living room, slipped into my shoes, sat on the same chair, and picked up my tea. Sofia made faces of conspiracy at me from the couch, as if we were kids playing a trick on playmates. I smiled back at her to leave her with her belief that I'd done that just for fun rather than to get information.

The door to the office jerked open, and the three men, led by Antonio who must have been the one rattling the doorknob, returned to the living room. A thundercloud surrounded my cousin, or might as well have, considering the closed, mutinous expression on his face.

His gaze landed on me with a roaring silent warning. Stay out of my way, it said.

Had I not known him most of my life, not saved him from a snake once, not shared so many pleasant moments with him, that expression would have scared me. Antonio suffered no fools, allowed no one to lie to him. But he went about finding out the truth like a bulldozer instead of like me, cajoling, asking gently, getting the other person to trust me so they'd tell me things.

Plus, the only investigations I'd gotten involved in were ones where my safety was at stake, or where I knew the people affected, knew things about them Antonio wouldn't understand, things happening around women who shopped at my store, who told me their deepest secrets sometimes.

Aurelia Gonzalez had been one of those women. My eyes teared at the thought of her being gone. Even if my life weren't in danger, I'd have felt compelled to figure out who'd done this to her.

No one messed with my tribe and got away with it.

What all these goings-on right now told me, though, is that, yes, Eduardo knew something about the skeleton in his garden.

But, what? What was it that he knew? I couldn't see him as a killer even though he seemed to be hiding something.

No sense trying to talk to Antonio now, and besides he was headed out the front door already, his silent sidekick close on his heels.

He didn't even say goodbye to Sofia and me. The man was on a quest and right now, he saw me as just an obstacle instead of as an asset.

CHAPTER 14

With a business to run, one I'd closed most of the morning to go to Sofia's uncle's house with her, I needed to get back to work. Some regulars would be puzzled and maybe even worried since my store being closed during business hours was unusual.

Sofia stayed with her uncle, promising to be at the store by no later than after *comida*. Lunch.

I ignored a call from Manuel, because, of course, Antonio must have told him that I'd been at the house where a skeleton had been found. And he'd most likely also told him he needed to stop me from getting into his business. I bristled at the thought.

But right now, I couldn't think about that. A murder had to be solved. Two, if I counted the skeleton. Three, if Ramon had also been murdered.

So much chaos, once again! And at the most important moment of my life.

Oh my goodness! My wedding! I had a fitting for my dress at this very minute. Just as the thought popped into my head, my phone dinged with the reminder alert.

Going to Eduardo's house messed up my whole day. The shop would have to stay closed until Sofia got there.

Josefina, my head seamstress, and her assistants were waiting for me right now at my workshop. They were all very busy keeping up with the orders that kept coming in from the upscale shops in town that sold my original designs. They had no time to wait on anyone, not even me, their *jefa*. Their boss. I texted Josefina that I was on my way.

Then, I thought of my dress. I created it by starting with a vintage Pierre Balmain from the fifties. I made the train removable to avoid ruining it while we did our *callejoneada* after the ceremony, the traditional walk through town with our guests.

With Manuel and I in the lead, we'd all follow behind bride and groom *Mojiganga*s, two people hidden inside tall papier mâché puppets dressed in wedding clothes.

Every now and again, the puppets would pirouette, or do a few dance moves. A *banda de viento*—a mariachi band—would play as they walked with us all. In addition, there would be a donkey pulling a cart that held bottles of tequila, which servers would pour into cups everyone had been given to wear around their necks. Traditionally, this walk occurred before the wedding, but to avoid drunkenness during our ceremony, Manuel and I opted to have it afterwards.

At the end of the walk, everyone who'd participated would disperse to find their own way to our family's hacienda. There, we'd celebrate our nuptials until the early morning hours.

Our wedding celebration would include three *mariachi* bands and a DJ to set the vibe later in the evening. Tables would groan under heaps of delicious food, flanked by specialty food carts. A gargantuan cake was set to take center stage, circled by much smaller cakes like ducklings around their mom. Blame it on Manuel's and my *mamá*, but we're talking a guest list of two hundred from the family alone. Throw in the hacienda staff, and we'd be nearing a crowd of three hundred!

Sometimes, I found it difficult to believe this was all about to happen. My wedding. To Manuel! Swoon, swoon, swoon.

As long as those men didn't have it in mind to do anything that could prevent me from getting there, that is ...

I walked to the corner of Canal and Hernandez Macias to meet my Uber. Just as I got in, tote (Dior Beige Multicolor) slung over my shoulder, I saw one of the sinister men walking in the direction of El Jardin. He strolled, just a person going about his day, as if he weren't a criminal, which, I now was certain, he was.

I frowned. Why was he still lurking around? Would one or the other continue stalking me forever?

While in the backseat of the car, finally with a bit of privacy, I removed the pieces of paper I'd retrieved from Eduardo's trash from my pockets and transferred them to the bottom of my tote. I'd look at them as soon as I got home from work. Right now, I had to concentrate on my dress.

I'd no sooner been dropped off in front of my workshop that my phone vibrated with a call. Manuel again. My finger hesitated over the screen for just a moment before I swiped to answer, and I couldn't help but smile seeing his name on the caller ID. "Manuel, *mi amor*, *hola*."

"Carli, *te quiero mucho*." I love you a lot.

My cheeks flushed and I felt tingly from my head to my toes. That man. Always knew how to get right to my core with his words, even simple ones like this.

"I love when you call me just to tell me that." I twirled a loose strand of hair around my finger, picturing his face.

"Ah, you know it was the first thing I called to say, but there's something else, too." He sighed loud enough for me to hear.

"What? What is it?" My grip tightened around the phone, while my shoulders tensed. My nerves felt so close to the surface already with everything going on, how could I handle more?

"Antonio said there's been a double murder. In La Lejona."

My hand slapped itself across my mouth all on its own. What was going on in my town? What!

"Manuel ... what, who ... I mean, what's going on, *mi amor*? Will we ever have some peace around here?" I began pacing the the foyer which I'd entered while we spoke, my voice rising higher with each word.

"Ah, Carlita. *Sí*, of course." He sounded like the voice of reason. "This has nothing to do with us. There are murders every day in every city in all the world." I heard him take a deep breath, as if that would reassure both of us.

I gagged on my own saliva thinking of my stalkers.

But, at least, this double murder could be left to Antonio and his colleagues. The chances of it being related to Aurelia and Ramon, and a skeleton, were remote.

"So, why are you telling me?" I twirled my hair around a finger, feeling suspicious about his call.

He waited a beat before answering. "Antonio said that he won't have much time to look into that skeleton, you know. It's been there a while, and it's more important to find who killed two men during the past twenty-four hours, and who killed Aurelia Gonzalez, and what happened to her husband." He almost didn't take a breath while saying all this.

Ah, he was telling me he knew I knew about the skeleton without telling me he knew I knew about it. Obviously, Antonio had reported that I'd been at Eduardo Caldera's house. And obviously, there was a message from Antonio in all this.

And, sure enough. "*Mi vida* (my life), you won't like this, but Antonio also asked me to tell you to not get involved."

"What do you mean?" My hackles rose realizing that Antonio thought he could tell me what to do or not to do through Manuel now that we'd be married. Well, newsflash for him. Manuel respected my independence. Unless it came to my safety. And, I supposed, this situation did involve my safety. Sigh.

What would they think if they knew about the two men stalking me? And what about what I felt had been a revelation coming from Sofia's uncle? And the pieces of paper now gathered like large confetti at the bottom of my tote?

I refocused on Manuel explaining Antonio's concerns.

"He just doesn't want you to get hurt, *mi amor*." He continued in a softer voice. "And I don't either ..."

My heart reached out to his. No doubt that when I got an idea in my head, not even Manuel could pull it out and quash it.

I told him to not worry, that I loved him more than I loved clothes, even—which always made him laugh—and we said goodbye.

Lifting my eyes toward the large, airy sewing room, I gazed at my wedding dress holding center stage on a mannequin. All other thoughts flew from my mind like birds scared off the trees in El Jardin by firecrackers.

My fitting went so well that nothing needed to be done to my dress other than a tweak around the waist.

The whole time, I couldn't help it, the Gonzalezes—Aurelia in particular—and the skeleton, all danced in my head. Just talking about my dilemmas out loud, often to my bio-father, helped me work them out. In most cases, though, nowadays it was Manuel I'd go to, or my mother. And Luna. I could talk to her about things I could not discuss with the others.

Like about how to solve a murder ...

I called my best friend while walking back to my shop, where I planned to only stop for a few minutes to check on things, and asked her to meet me at El Café.

On my way there, I took time to admire two unusual front doors. Doing so always lifted my mood.

One towered at twenty feet, and was stunning, a thick slab of hand-carved wood with bits of color here and there. The other one was a mere seven feet high but equally eye-catching, with its vibrant blue color against the building's ochre and the realistic, colorful birds carved into it.

As I approached the coffee shop, I saw Luna arriving from the opposite direction.

In no time at all, we were seated on one of the couches in the covered section of the courtyard patio. Luna leaned toward me as I told her all that had transpired at Eduardo's house, about the torn paper I'd taken, and all that I knew about the Gonzalezes, and the men following me, and about Manuel and I having found my rooftop deck door open.

"Well, wow, *chica*, that's a lot." She took a sip of her drink, looking at me the whole time. I nodded at her.

"And the first thing is, do you even want to think about that stuff right now? Why not turn those pieces of paper over to Antonio?"

I gazed at her while the hum of conversations and sounds from the street just outside the courtyard buzzed around us.

"But ... but, what if there isn't a big day unless I do something?" I leaned toward her while twirling a strand of my hair.

Luna looked at me, lips pursed, eyes thoughtful, as if she were looking for an answer in mine. Something seemed to click for her, and she went into analyzing mode. That was Luna, spontaneous and changeable like shadows across the moon.

"So, it seems the skeleton could be Eduardo's missing cousin." She stated.

"Yes," I agreed.

"It makes sense, actually, since he disappeared long ago, *sí*?"

"I don't know. It can take just a few months for a body to decompose when it's buried like that. Without being embalmed,

I mean. We can assume no one embalmed someone buried in a garden ..."

"How do you know that? About a body, I mean. Manuel?"

I shook my head no. "Ms. Google told me."

We giggled about that like the schoolgirls we'd once been, sharing different secrets right here on this patio.

We then both took a sip of our drinks. And I thought ... what a sad way to be at the end of one's life. A skeleton, hidden in a garden. No funeral, no loved ones to pray over you, ignored on Día de los Muertos—the Day of the Dead, the joyous holiday when the spirit of loved ones returned to visit their families. None of that for this poor soul. Of course, he, or she, might have been a bad person ...

"Ah, Carli, let's just forget this whole thing, *sí?* Let's focus on your wedding."

I shrugged. "I don't have to focus on it all that much, you know that. Mamá is doing everything. My job is to take care of the dress and show up when I'm required. And the dress is done. As of this morning." I grinned at her.

She knew my mom well, so this broke the tension and we laughed, clinking our paper cups.

Just as we finally relaxed into the beautiful afternoon and one another's company, one of the men who'd been following me came into the courtyard from the El Café side, and without looking at me, walked across it and left by the street exit.

My body tensed, and, discreetly, I gripped Luna's hand. She, who caught on quickly to things, said nothing until the man disappeared from view.

"That was him, right? I mean, one of them? From this morning?"

I nodded.

She said, "I'll come help you put the pieces of paper together," as she gripped my hand back.

CHAPTER 15

M anuel and I had decided to make tonight's dinner about last-minute decisions regarding our honeymoon and wedding weekend, since we'd missed out on the planning the night Ramon died.

We'd be eating at Manuel's Eatery, which meant walking by the Parroquia and El Jardin to get there. Just as well, I couldn't let what had happened to Ramon spoil the joy strolling around our square brought me. After all, I was getting married in that church in just a few days.

I gazed over the food carts that lined the small park on two sides, serving local favorites like *nieves*—ice cream, tacos, and in the evening, *esquites*, corn off the cobb, served in a cup and covered with mayonnaise, cheese, and *chile* powder. The mouth-watering smells traveled through the air, olfactory pied pipers drawing the crowd to the carts.

I'd always liked this scene and did my best to enjoy it now while keeping vigilant for anyone following me. My heart beat harder as I thought about how Manuel would react if he knew about those two men. Or rather, about the fact I didn't tell him about them ...

Why come into my shop for a gift certificate? It couldn't be a coincidence that they'd started to come around after I'd seen Balaclava Man and called the police. I, at least, felt certain that these two things were related.

Just as they popped into my mind, I saw them, standing by a bench in El Jardín, one of them holding an ice cream cone. I froze in my tracks, my eyes on the men.

Shockingly, standing with them, *arguing* with them, was a familiar figure. Pablo Ortega, the husband of Ramon and Aurelia's daughter, Leonora. It was him, *sí*? My eyes squinted, doubting for just a second. I hadn't seen him for a couple of years, but, yes, that was him—looked too much like him to be anyone else.

It dawned on me that he, also, had the same build and hair color as Balaclava Man. Could it be ...? My mind stalled at the thought.

The tension between the three men was so palpable, I could feel it despite the distance. And I noticed people meandering about the park glancing their way. One of the men with Pablo stood next to him, arms crossed, a scowl on his face. Pablo also crossed his arms, while the one with the ice cream angrily threw his cone into a nearby trash can, his gestures getting even more animated afterward.

Just then, a *mariachi* band that had been setting up in that corner of the park struck the first chord. All three men turned toward the music, giving me the perfect chance to remain unnoticed, to slip away, head down, praying none of them turned my way.

What was the Gonzalezes' son-in-law doing talking to criminals? Did he have something to do with what had happened
to Aure ... no, I refused to think it.
I turned the corner onto Umarán, fixing my eyes ahead toward
Manuel's Eatery.

Taking a deep breath, I tucked away my worries so Manuel
wouldn't see them etched on my face.

But ... could I hide this from him? Should I?

CHAPTER 16

The next morning, craving normalcy, I made it a point to go through my matcha ritual exactly as usual before everything happened.

For a moment, I allowed my heart to sing, and did not think about the latest events. I watched Dap rolling himself on the ground in a spot of sunshine on the roof deck.

"Dapperoo, I love you," I crooned.

His tail thumping against the ground, he gave me a look as if he wondered about the truth of that, me, the one who didn't always give him all the treats he wanted, and who wouldn't let him sit on her chest when she lay in bed, the one who left the house every day and didn't take him with her.

I chuckled to myself, but my thoughts soon returned to the puzzle of the deaths, and the two men whom I now thought of as The Followers because they seemed to be everywhere I went. And now, Pablo, the son-in-law, apparently involved with them.

I felt my eyes glisten, remembering happy times spent with Ramon and Aurelia, their thirty-fifth anniversary party, their daughter's engagement, my interactions with Aurelia at my shop. They now seemed like sad memories to me.

Last night, I'd somehow managed to keep many things from Manuel by pushing our conversation to our honeymoon. We had decided on Hawaii, a place neither of us had ever been.

Though I wasn't lying to him—I was only holding back information—it bothered me. A lot. So why was I doing it? Because he would do all he could to stop me. And I'd have to rely on Antonio to figure this whole thing out ... before my wedding. Unacceptable.

My phone vibrated on the table next to me, dancing a little on the glass top.

Looking at the display screen, I realized I was about to keep everything I knew from one more person. Antonio.

"Antonio, *hola*!"

"Hola Carli. *¿Cómo va todo?"* How's everything.

"Oh, you know. A bunch of murders before my wedding. My cousin Antonio instructing my fiancé on what I can and cannot do. You know, the usual."

"Carli ..." He dragged out my name, exasperation in his voice.

"Urgh ... trying to tell me what to do by proxy!" My nostrils flared and my heart beat faster.

"I'm the detective here, *prima*, not you," he said, his tone as sharp as the edge of one of Manuel's chef's knives.

"Yes, but if my life is in danger, then I get to be involved, *vato*!" Dude.

"Wait. Why do you think your life is in danger?" His words pierced through the phone line with unmistakable alertness.

My face flushed. Now, he knew that something was going on besides me seeing Balaclava Man. Why, why, why had I said that!

"Well ... well, you know. That man, Antonio. He knows where I live."

I held my breath, fingers crossed that he would believe I only feared Balaclava Man. A deep sigh came through the line. I relaxed, at least until he spoke again.

"I have someone watching your house to make sure no one is trying to go in—Manuel told me about your door being opened." He paused, as if waiting for me to apologize for not telling him about that myself. I hoped for his sake that he wasn't holding his breath. He gave up and continued, "And you don't know that he knows you saw him. You assume!"

I took in a sharp breath, putting aside for a moment that Balaclava Man had to know that I'd seen him and called the police. *Antonio had people on me?*

"You did? I mean, you do? Still? Have people watching me?" The reality of that sank in. I'd have to be extra careful where I went in case they also followed me.

"Yes. I take the safety of my favorite cousin seriously," he said, warmth in his voice. "Plus, you're an important witness. If it turns out the man you saw did it, I mean."

"Hmm ... did Manuel put you up to that?" I frowned, suspicious.

"Carli, why does it bother you that Manuel and me, we want to make sure you're safe?" He sounded frustrated.

I shrugged, then realized he couldn't see me.

"Okay, I get it. Why did you call?" I rolled my eyes.

A deep sigh came through. "I wanted to let you know that we know the cause of death of Aurelia Gonzalez."

I sat straight up at this, prompting Dap to lift his head and look at me. I dashed inside as cars in front of my house started honking, not unusual for this area, and I didn't want to miss a word. Now, I stood just inside, behind the closed door that led to the roof.

"And?" I held my breath.

He seemed to hesitate, then just said it. "Suffocation." I felt his weariness.

Tears came to my eyes. Poor Aurelia ...

"Oh ... so, someone would have had to do that, *si*? It wouldn't happen on its own. I mean, like Aurelia did it by accident?" As I said it, I realized the impossibility of that.

"No. Only babies die of suffocation by accident." He sounded tired, either from all the work, or from the constant harm he saw people inflict on one another. I did feel badly for him about all the ugliness of life he saw every day in his work. He cleared his throat as if getting ready to say something else.

Before he could speak, the bells at the Parroquia began to toll. I'd walked back out onto the roof deck, but now re-entered the house.

"And something else," continued Antonio.

I held my breath in anticipation, heart pounding, and waited for him to continue. I didn't want anything I said to stop him now that he seemed willing to confide at least this much in me.

"Aurelia's wedding and engagement rings weren't on her finger. Do you know anything about them?" He coughed. "Wait, I need water." He was silent for a moment, during which the distinct crack of a water bottle cap being opened reached my ears. Then, he continued. "The Gonzalez children will all be here by this evening, and I could ask them, but I know you saw her often enough. Do you remember if she always wore them?"

Well, I knew of at least one Gonzalez "child" who must already be here if she'd come with her husband, and the thought of Pablo distracted me from Antonio's question, but then I caught myself.

"Oh. Yes, yes, I think so ..." I closed my eyes, picturing Aurelia's hands, trying hard to remember if she'd always had them on whenever I saw her.

"Yes, she did, I'm pretty sure."

"Okay, thank you. Another thing for me to figure out, pfft." He released another sigh. My heart ached for him in this moment.

"Anyway," he added, soothing, caring Antonio making an appearance. "I just wanted to let you know about her. Just don't go spreading it around!" He said, as if frustrated with me for something I hadn't even done yet, and might never do. Plus, when did I ever spread news "around," other than in our immediate small group"

I ignored that. And yes, I'd wanted to know about Aurelia, but also ... "Antonio. What about Eduardo?" I held my breath.

"Ah. We still don't have the result of his autopsy. A different coroner was assigned, and he had others to do first. He's supposed to have an answer for us by tomorrow."

"It's taking so long!" Impatience crept into my voice.

"He just died on Wednesday, Carli ..."

"*Sí*, of course. So, they'll release the bodies at the same time, then?"

"*Sí*. That's the plan, at least." I heard voices behind him and his muffled response.

I thought of the vigil that was sure to start once the children were all here. I'd go, of course. Would Pablo be there? I shook the thought away. Of course, Carlota Maria Garcia Cano, he'll be there. He's the son-in-law!

Then, I froze, eyes wide, looking at nothing. Would Pablo bring those men, my followers, to the vigil? A shiver ran down my spine.

While that went through my mind, not really registering what Antonio was saying about the vigil and funeral, I grabbed my now empty teacup, made my way down to the kitchen, and placed it in the sink.

"Carli? Are you there? What else is going on? You're not keeping something from me?" His tone was now more abrupt. Antonio knew me well enough to sense I wasn't being completely up front.

A blush crept up my face. This was it. I had to tell him everything. But if I did, he'd get in the way of my investigation!

Yet ... *he* was the detective, I reminded myself.

I grabbed a strand of hair from my ponytail and twirled it between the fingers of my left hand and barely breathed, like one who knows a horrific thing is about to happen, like seeing a bomb coming down from the sky right above her, or someone standing in front of her with a gun, or ... any manner of nefariousness about to get her.

I took a deep breath.

"Maybe?" I mumbled into the phone. It came out in a croak, while the phone slipped in my now sweaty hand.

"CARLI? *¿Cómo te atreves?*" He huffed. "How dare you?" He repeated in English. "After everything we said? Never mind! I'm going to your house!" Like a petulant boy, he added, "And, AND, I'm bringing your fiancé!" He hung up without saying goodbye, the equivalent of slamming down an old-fashioned house phone.

Urgh. I rolled my eyes, something I seemed to do a lot around Antonio these past few days. How to get myself out of this one?

Before I'd even had time to put my cup into the dishwasher, the doorbell rang. Must be Antonio, because I'd given Manuel a key with permission to use it as if he already lived here. Manuel would be so angry ...

My heart hammered in my chest. The doorbell went off again before I could make it down to the first floor. I watched Dap closely, always fearing his curiosity would one day lead him to slip between my legs and out the front door. No matter what he believed, my boy wasn't ready for the outside world.

"Realmente, Antonio, give me a second! You wanted me to run down here and break my neck on the stairs?" I asked as I slung the door open.

He stood, a deep scowl on his face, eyes hooded, murder in them, not saying a word.

I deflated like a hot air balloon after landing.

Cocking my head toward the top of the stairs, I decided, was enough of an invitation for him to follow me in.

We spoke not a word on our way up. I headed to the kitchen so I could put the island between us.

I leaned back against the sink, looking at him, unable to prevent my arms from crossing. I hoped it would hide my shaking hands from him.

I opened my mouth to say something, but just then, I heard the front door open and Manuel calling out that he was here.

He headed straight for me, which meant the island also separated him from Antonio.

"*¿Qué pasa?*" He looked from me to Antonio and back again. What's going on.

Antonio had still not said a word, squinting at me instead. His only response to Manuel's question was to glance at him and give one nod in my direction, his way of indicating that only I knew the answer.

Manuel, his arm around my shoulders, turned toward me. "Carlita?" He asked, his voice gentle.

"Well, *sabes*?" You know.

"NO! We don't know, which is why we're asking!" The words exploded out of Antonio's mouth, as if out of an underground mine.

"*¡Oye, carnal!* Why are you talking to my wife like that?" Manuel tensed next to me, a hundred and eighty pounds of muscle waiting to pounce on trouble. My whole being lit up at his defense of me. Listen brother.

"She's not your wife yet," said Antonio, deadpan, not looking remorseful at all for talking to me in such a nasty tone of voice, one I assumed he used on the criminals he arrested every day.

Manuel stared at him a moment; we both did. The atmosphere in the kitchen held so much tension that Dap took off for my bedroom, letting out a plaintive meow on the way.

"She will be in just a few days." He said, his voice so low, yet with so much power behind it that no one could mistake that he wouldn't stand for Antonio using that tone of voice with me.

The last thing I wanted was to see two of my favorite people in the whole world get into a fist fight over me.

"*VATOS*! No fighting, please. I ... I'll tell you what's happening." I cringed in anticipation of their reaction.

Manuel turned his murderous gaze from Antonio to me, disbelief and wonder joining the anger on his face. My heart sank. Would I lose him for breaking my promise?

"Should I make coffee first?" I asked, trying to sound casual, but feeling like a butterfly storm was raging in my stomach.

They both answered with a resounding "NO!" at the very same time.

"Well, can we at least go sit on the couch?" I needed to be in my favorite place to think, with Dap on my lap, though he wasn't about to come into the living room considering the level of tension in the air.

Again, the answer was a collective resounding "No!"

With both of them staring at me, I cleared my throat and began, frantically trying to figure out—on the spur of the moment—whether to tell them everything. Or not.

"So, okay. On the day I saw Balaclava Man com ..."

"Who?" Barked Antonio.

It's then that I realized I'd never called him that in front of either Antonio or Manuel.

"You know, the man who came out of the Gonzalez house, that I saw, wearing one." I twisted the fringe of a dishcloth, pretending a calmness I didn't feel.

Antonio pursed his lips at my explanation. I could tell he might, just might, be trying to suppress a smile at the nick-name I'd given the man.

Manuel looked at me, disappointment, and fear in his eyes, but also kindness. The emotions displayed on his face in rapid succession like a film on fast-forward.

But, by now he'd picked up on the fact that I'd been lying to him by not telling him what I was about to say.

Yet ..., something stopped me from telling them everything.

"Well, when I was walking to your place for dinner last night, *mi amor*, I saw one of the sons-in-law of the Gonzalezes, Pablo Ortega, in El Jardin talking to two men who looked, well, they looked like thugs. They were all arguing, and it was noticeable enough that many people were staring at them. That's all." I finished in a murmur, looking down, not daring to look either of them in the eye.

"Are you *loca*, Carli?" Nearly yelled Antonio. Crazy.

"¡Vato!" Said Manuel. I didn't even need to see his eyes to feel the warning in them.

Antonio stood taller and crossed his arms tighter. "You see that after seeing what who probably a murderer coming out of his in-laws' house, now the scene of a crime, and you think it's okay to not tell me?" If smoke could come out of a human's ears ...

"¡Basta!" Said Manuel, so much caution and restraint in just one word. Enough.

Antonio stared at him for a moment, breathing fast, looking undecided about how to take that. The machismo way by using his cop authority, or acting like our cousin and giving me a chance to explain. The cousin won.

"Have you seen any of them since?" He asked, looking first at Manuel, then at me, the storm still raging in his eyes.

I could see that was berating himself for having only had my house watched instead of also having me followed. Something I did not want him to start doing at all. How could I get around town if that happened? I'd have to use all sorts of ways to disguise myself and to lose whoever he assigned to the task.

"No, I mean, it was just that one time." It wasn't a lie. Not really. I'd never seen Pablo with The Followers before, or since.

"Carlita, *querida* ... why didn't you say something?" Manuel asked in a too-normal tone of voice.

I trembled inside. "Well, it's nothing. I didn't want you to worry, *mi amor*."

Antonio held a look of momentous disbelief as his moustache kept moving because his mouth was in constant motion, as one trying hard to chew through disturbing information.

Finally, restraining himself, he spoke. "Can you describe them?" He cleared his throat.

I shrugged and gave him brief descriptions, not so much that he'd realize I had to have seen them more than once, and close up at that, instead of from the distance of walking along the street next to the Jardin.

"You're not holding anything else back?" Antonio asked, his facial expression making it clear he wouldn't believe any answer I gave him.

Manuel said nothing, but stared at me, deep in thought. I could see he wanted to believe I'd never lie to him, but had doubts.

And I would never ... just, at times, a woman had to do what a woman had to do to keep her world in balance. Even if it included a white lie or two.

Okay, maybe a bit of a dark one every now and then, when necessary ...

CHAPTER 17

After Manuel and Antonio had left, leaving me with most of my secrets, I went to my shop to assist Esme and Sofia since Saturdays tended to be busy.

I returned home in the early evening to change for the vigil that I'd been told had started at the Gonzalezes. I dressed somberly in a dark tunic, opaque tights, and flat Ferragamo ankle boots. The occasion would be marked by an unusual absence—Ramon and Aurelia's bodies. Normally, they'd be lying in repose as customary for Mexican wakes, but their bodies were still at the morgue.

The vigil, as in many vigils in Mexico, would be a happy affair. Guests would share stories, laughter would resound, and lots of photos of the deceased, surrounded by lit candles, would be found all around, but especially on an altar created wherever everyone was sure to see it.

As for the *velorio*—the funeral—that would have to wait until the release of the bodies which would be who knew when, what with Aurelia having been killed.

Manuel couldn't come with me tonight, and besides, he'd never met the Gonzalez family. Though as my fiancé, he had every right to come along, and I'd have asked him to accompany me. Except he'd have known in an instant if I was doing more than just paying my respects.

Dap, who could tell I would soon be leaving him again, twirled himself like a ribbon around my legs as I stood in my closet, attempting to put on tights.

"Dap, no," I said, voice firm. He ignored me until I nudged him away with my foot. Offended, he slunk off in the direction of the bedroom, giving me his *you're rude* meow as he went. My heart pinched a little, but his behavior also made me smile.

I left my house and walked all the way around the corner and to the Gonzalez home. The courtyard doors were wide open, and several cars were parked on its paved surface. I guessed that Leonora and Alejandro had driven in from their respective homes in Mexico City and Guanajuato.

The front door of the house was open, and a man in a high-quality long-sleeved black t-shirt and black pants stood there as if guarding the entrance. Which he most likely was, considering the situation.

I greeted him and after checking that I belonged, he let me in.

The first person I saw was Leonora, looking subdued. She stood in the foyer, gazing at a large photo of her parents on the wall.

"Leonora?" I asked, keeping my voice low to match her somber mood.

She turned and stared at me for a moment, as if unsure of who I was. She caught herself quickly and leaned to kiss me on both cheeks.

"Carli, *gracias para por venir.*" Thank you for coming.

"Por supuesto." Of course. I offered her my heartfelt condolences and she hugged me this time, tears in her eyes.

We talked for a few minutes, then her brother, Alejandro, came up to us to re-introduce himself; I knew him from the parties at the Gonzalez home, too, but we hadn't talked much, what with both events having had several dozen people attending.

Before I knew it, all three of Ramon and Aureli's children surrounded me, asking questions about what had happened to their father in El Jardin. And Graciela, the youngest, spoke about how her mother loved the game of selling her designer clothes through my shop.

No one said anything about me seeing Balaclava Man, so Antonio must not have shared that with them. Did they know how their mother had died? Did they know she'd been smothered?

Just then, Pablo joined us. He introduced himself to me, looking all innocent. As if he hadn't met with criminals in our Jardin, as if oblivious to it.

"Hola Carli, *mucho gusto,"* he said. Pleased to meet you.

I reminded him that we'd already met, at his engagement party several years ago, and he acknowledged that. I hadn't gone to the wedding because I'd been in New York City by then, hard at work in my internship.

Then, Leonora explained to him that I'd been with Eduardo at the time he died. I watched him for a negative reaction, but his only response was to nod once with lips pursed. He pulled his wife close, and kissed her on the head.

"Pablo, I'm so sorry that you lost both your in-laws so soon, so close together," I said, mustering all the goodwill I could, just in case I got the purpose of his meeting with The Followers wrong. He seemed calmer than a man involved in a crime related to his recently deceased in-laws should be.

The conversation continued between me and the Gonzalezes and their spouses, all of us eventually moving into the dining room where food had been laid out, *jalapeño* poppers, mini *quesadillas*, miniature frittatas in muffin cups, and other food that could be eaten standing up, which it seemed everyone was doing. The scent of all the flavors filled the air, making my mouth water, as I hadn't eaten since *comida*.

By then, many more mourners had arrived, and some gathered in small groups, whispering to each other, leaning in close and occasionally casting quick, furtive glances at Ramon and Aurelia's children. It was evident from their behavior that they were aware of the unnatural circumstances surrounding Aurelia's death.

Were any of them involved? I wondered.

Quiet music played in the background, piano, some Viennese waltzes, which would be surprising if one didn't know about the Gonzalezes' love of classical music.

Out of the corner of my eye, I observed Pablo, who, over the past few minutes, had meandered to the periphery of our group. A moment later, he looked down at his phone, and his head snapped up as if searching for something, his eyes landing on the entrance to the hallway that led to the bedrooms. He headed that way as he answered, his demeanor making it clear that he wasn't happy with whomever was on the call, but I seemed to be the only one who noticed.

Remembering that the guest bathroom was also located down that hallway, I gave it five seconds, then excused myself from the group, and followed him into the hallway.

I reached the bathroom without seeing him, and assumed I'd lost my chance to hear his conversation. But just as I was about to close the bathroom door, I heard him speak. I realized he was just on the other side of the partially open door of the room across the hallway. I leaned my ear to the bathroom door, left slightly ajar.

And my eyes bugged out at what I heard. Pablo was definitely unhappy with whomever was on the line with him.

I concentrated hard on what he was saying to be certain I missed nothing. His voice, tense and angry, came through clear enough. "*Ella es ... ella era mi suegra. Mi esposa la adoraba ...* " His voice sounded full of anger, but also regret. She was my mother-in-law. My wife adored her ...

I swallowed the phantom golf ball that had formed in my throat and did my best to control the nausea that overcame me.

CHAPTER 18

I closed the bathroom door, making not a sound, and splashed water on my face, reminding myself to breathe, and slowing my heart rate as best I could.

As soon as possible, I returned to the Gonzalez living room, Pablo's words prominent on my mind like an in-your-face billboard. What I'd heard and what it might mean consumed me.

Just then, my phone buzzed with a text from Luna.

I can go now, to do the journal pages?

Yes!

I wanted to see her even more now, to share this new development. So I said my goodbyes, and made my exit.

As I walked back home, like a haunting echo, I kept hearing Pablo saying, in a voice that betrayed shock and horror, *"She's ... she was my mother-in-law. My wife adored her."*

What could he have meant? It's as if he'd been talking to the killer ... and if that was the case, then he hadn't it done it, right?

I tried to shake those thoughts and the confusing chill they brought. I couldn't wait to see Luna. Together, we'd figure this whole thing out, I decided.

Once home, I opened a bottle of Cabernet, the cork coming out with a soft hiss, and got two glasses. Luna would want some, and I did, too. I poured, and the wine glugged into the glasses, the rich, fruity aroma filling the air.

I plopped myself onto the couch, and seconds later, Dap jumped on my lap, letting out a wistful meow. He gave me a look that said I was too often gone.

"Qué pasa in our world, Dapperoo?" What's going on.

I leaned back against the plush couch cushions, allowing my distress over Aurelia and Ramon to flow through me, and petted Dap. He purred, a soothing rumble that eased my tension.

For some reason, my mind meandered to my Jiu Jitsu classes, which I'd put on hold. I now knew enough to defend myself and do it well in case of attack. Other things had been more important lately, me never thinking I might need those skills again since, remember, no more sleuthing for me.

But I recalled my teacher saying that things weren't always as they seemed—as if I needed a reminder—but why had that come to mind now? My mind wandered back to Pablo.

In no time, I heard the new Ring doorbell that Manuel had installed the day before. I got up and skirted by the kitchen to look at the camera. I smiled seeing Luna by my door, and skipped down the stairs to let her in.

We hugged and she followed me upstairs, her heels clicking rhythmically on the steps.

On the way up, she asked, "So, *chica*, any news on anything?"

I motioned her forward with a flourish. "Well, some things, but upstairs first!"

"Got some wine? I hope?"

Now on the second floor, I turned to her and pointed at myself with mock surprise, "Luna, duh, it's me you're visiting. On a Saturday night ... hello?"

Her laughter bubbled up as she playfully tossed her hair back. "Lead the way to it, then!"

Dap came up to her, and as usual, she sneaked him a treat. With no cats of her own, she showered love on mine.

"You going to make my cat fat," I said, giving a pretend pout.

"Pfft ..." came the response from my big, beautiful friend who never saw a *quesadilla* she didn't devour with relish.

My turn to laugh.

We settled onto the couch and as I poured the wine, Luna leaned forward, eyes sparkling with curiosity. I told her about Pablo's phone conversation, and we tried to figure out who he might have been talking to. And what he had meant.

I pondered the situation aloud, twirling the wine glass in my hand, "If it was an admission, why would the killer admit to it, over the phone, no less?"

Unable to come up with answers that made sense, we turned to the torn pages of the diary. Taking them from their hiding place in my closet, I laid them across my dining room table, first putting Dap in the bedroom so he didn't mess them up.

"So, you think this is linked to Aurelia Gonzalez, *sí*?" Asked Luna, as she sat herself at the table.

"Yes. No. Urgh, *no se*, Luna." I said, joining her. I don't know.

"Well, *chica*, gotta figure it out. I want to help, okay?"

I smiled at her, feeling grateful. "I'm completely lost, so thank you."

"Well, let's get to it, then. So, you think Ramon was killed, too?" Her brow furrowed.

I shrugged, giving a dismissive wave of my head, as if that explained things.

Luna took a contemplative sip of wine, her gaze fixed on the jigsaw of paper before us. She picked up a piece, holding it up to the light, then with a slight frown, put it back down, shaking her head.

The sound of horns and conversations buzzing on the street below reached us. We remained silent, thinking our own thoughts while we worked on the puzzle. There were still so many pieces, it was difficult to tell how many pages there were, but I thought it was five or six. With writing on both sides. What would they disclose?

So far, we had about a quarter of one page, and about half of another, and just a corner of a third with no writing on it. What with sips of wine, and stretching and talking about other things too, progress was slow.

"Luna, let's focus," I said, unable to keep myself from being distracted and laughing as she told me a funny story about one of her website clients.

Soon, we had another quarter page. We both felt disappointed that we'd been unable to get even one full page by now. Still, we did learn something important.

A partial page said this: "*Also, there is my family's investment. If*" –and here a big chunk of paper was missing—then continued with "*everyone involved ...*" and then another missing piece. Then, on what was the bottom of the page, which we knew because of the straight edge of the paper—it went on to say, "*is the matter of that investment*," then more missing paper. So frustrating!

"Let's see what the other side looks like," said Luna, leaning forward.

We turned the page over. At the top, it said, "*my family*," and then again "*the buildings cost so much to ...*" Then, what was about four of five lines lower, it said "*We are pulling*" then, after another gap, "*because what if the police discover that his father ...*"

Pulling what? Whose father? Whose family? What buildings?

"Argh, this makes me crazy!" I exclaimed, pushing back from the table with a huff, my chair scraping against the floor. I grabbed my entire ponytail and twirled it.

"I know! Me too!" Retorted Luna, her eyes roaming over the dozens more pieces.

I sat back down and looked at what we had so far. About halfway down a page, past a big hole, it read "*Colonia San Antonio*," then another gap, and then "*..ht studio apartments suitable for ... market, ... nomads.*"

Was he talking about a real estate investment? By now, I felt convinced that this was Eduardo's journal. No reason. Just a gut feeling, which often turned out right.

I looked at the second side of the other partial page we had.

"the whole family ...," and then, *"to be discov...",* and later *"Alberto."*

"Ah! We have a name. FINALLY!" Said-shouted Luna.

Despite my frustration and the information not coming fast enough for me, I smiled at Luna's reaction.

"Yep, that we do, *chica*!"

We just had to keep putting the fragments together. Patiently.

Then, I remembered something. I took a sharp breath, my eyes opening wide.

"Oh, Luna!" I exclaimed.

She looked back at me, startled, her mouth in an O.

CHAPTER 19

"*What?*" Said Luna, startled by my exclamation.

"I forgot, oh, how could I?" I flapped my hands in the air.

She turned to me, eyebrows raised in question.

"Wait here!" I said and scurried to my closet. I grabbed a bag from my shop, Carli's Secret Closet imprinted in pink across the front of the shiny white bag, and headed back to the living room.

"What is it?" Luna asked, toying with her bottom lip as soon as I appeared with the bag.

I lifted my eyes to the sky as if exasperated, but smiled at my friend's impatience.

"What it is ..." I mimicked a drum roll with my hands, "is this!"

I handed her the bag ceremoniously.

Looking at me suspiciously, she opened it, and, as if lifting a Fabergé egg from its crate, she pulled out a shoe box with the Jimmy Choo logo on it. She looked at me, frowning.

"Let's go over there," she said, nodding in the direction of the living room, as she got up. "So we don't mess this up," meaning our puzzle.

Once we settled on the couch, she opened the box which contained a delicious pair of Jimmy Choo Baily 100 stilettos covered in crystals and pearls. A true work of art. And a perfect match to Luna's lavender and very light grey maid of honor dress.

"Ooh, Carli ... these are *new* ... they must have cost *una fortuna*!" She said, wonder in her voice. She pulled one shoe out of the box, held it up to the light, and stared.

I stared, too, at the magnificence before realizing what she'd said. "Ha! That's for me to know." I replied, closing my lips hard, smiling. She'd scream if she knew the price.

She sighed like someone who regrets something that hasn't even happened yet.

"*¿Qué?*" I asked, surprised she wasn't jumping for joy at this incredible work of art she'd get to wear on her feet.

"Chica, I'm not wearing these heels at your wedding." She said, putting the shoe back into the box, shaking her head, as if at a naughty child who'd broken a rule.

"What? Why not?" I asked, shocked. I touched her hand.

She looked at me and smiled, eyes glistening.

"Mi amor, you're the bride. I'm not going to tower over you with those things." She nodded in the direction of the shoes. I glanced at them, then back at her, confused.

"You should be the tallest female in our group as we stand at the altar while you marry the love of your life." She said it as if afraid to wake the tiger in her that would want to take the words back so she could wear the shoes.

I stared at my best friend, dumbfounded. Luna never, ever, hardly ever, went anywhere without heels, despite her five-foot-eight height. I often said she was as tall as a palm tree, but with the girth of an oak.

My heart flip-flopped in my chest. I batted my eyes to avoid spilling tears.

"Oh, Luna, no, argh ... my mascara is running," I said as I ran a finger under each eye.

She laughed from deep in her belly, which made me smile and laugh, too.

I fell onto the couch next to her, each of us turning toward the other. She took my hand and we sat there, looking at one another, two friends enjoying a moment made precious by her generosity, my unbounded love for her, hers for me, and by the momentous prospect of my upcoming nuptials to Manuel, something that, just a few months ago, had seemed impossible. Just impossible.

I stared at the shoes, sparkling as they peeked out of their box.

"Chula, you should wear them," Luna said with reverence, as if just trying on the idea herself. Cutie.

"Me?"

It had never occurred to me. I already had the perfect pair of Valentinos, but then, in my mind's eye, I saw these shoes next to my dress and realized that they were a perfect fit.

"Ah, really?" I asked.

She assented, her eyes huge and glistening.

I loved this woman, my best friend forever. My sister.

"Wait, what will you wear?"

She patted my hand. "Don't you worry about that. You can see on the morning of."

"What?" I said, surprised she'd keep that from me.

"You'll see. I already got them; they're beautiful and I know you'll love them." She smiled, smirked more like it, and added. "After the wedding, I'm consigning them with you, because, of course, I'll never wear them again. Such tiny heels, ha ha!" She held her hand up, fingers splayed, to emphasize her general disdain for low-heeled shoes. I burst into laughter, and she joined me.

We returned to the dining room table, and forty minutes later we had a third incomplete page and a few more pieces taped to the first two. What we both wanted was at least one full page so we could see if any of it would lead to the truth of anything.

We bent over the new partial page to read what it said, a challenging task as it was taped together in so many places that the overlapping layers obscured our view.

His handwriting was a bit difficult to decipher, making our job harder. Still, what it said soon became clear.

Luna grabbed my right arm with her left and we turned toward each other.

"That's crazy," I murmured. She nodded, wariness in her eyes. I held my breath and saw Luna doing the same.

"... *if the body was discovered by the ...* " and after another gap, "*had deposited some funds into the bank account...* " And again "*not just his father's money.*"

No wonder these pages had been thrown away. But, still, who had done what? Whose father was he talking about? Was it about the skeleton in the backyard or someone else? Were Ramon and Aurelia somehow involved in this?

Chapter 20

That night, I tossed and turned a lot, kept partially awake by a vivid dream. In it, I saw the back of a man bent over a female form on a bed, the legs, a nightgown twisted around them, kicking vigorously like that of a drowning person attempting to propel themselves back up to the surface of a swimming pool, or lake, or ocean. The man struggled to keep something on this female's face, and I knew it to be a pillow, though I couldn't quite see because his body was blocking it.

Yet, though I couldn't see their faces, I *knew* the woman to be Aurelia, and the male to be Balaclava Man. The way we *know* things in dreams. The legs stilled, and the man began to turn around toward me as if he felt my presence.

That's when I woke up in a sweat, my heart beating wildly, a full-blown anxiety attack, well, attacking me. Rain was pounding on my bedroom window. I took several deep breaths. Dap came from the foot of the bed and with a short, low meow, he hugged up by my side, purring away as if he thought it would calm me. It helped.

The clock on my bedside table read 3:03 a.m. It came to me that the man in my dream had the same body type as Pablo, which was the same as Balaclava Man, something I hadn't wanted to admit before despite my suspicions.

So, I believed that my dream had confirmed who had killed Aurelia.

Pablo ...

Because now, I felt convinced that he was Balaclava Man. Convinced. Yet, despite that, something seemed to be missing. Something I should see, but did not. Because then it made his phone conversation even more confusing.

And I couldn't go to Antonio and tell him he should arrest Pablo because of my dream.

Then, I recalled that The Followers also had that same body type. And dark hair of more or less the same length. I groaned.

I tried to go back to sleep, but after an hour, I gave up and meandered to the dining room where Luna and I had left our "puzzle," anticipating we'd work on it today. Depending on how that went, I might make an excuse to not go to Sunday *comida* at the hacienda, a tradition.

I stared at all the pieces of paper for a while, then saw how one of the larger loose ones might connect to a partial page. And sure enough, they fit together perfectly.

When I saw what it said, my heart began to beat so fast, I thought it would burst out of my chest and run away.

"... alf-rose from his seat, and reached for the bottle of tequila. He was singing, too loud, to a pop song, I forgot which because I was so drunk by then ..."

Who was he talking about? The slow progress frustrated me.

A bit lower on the page, he'd written, *"... just before it happened. Oh mi dio ... I could have stopped it, but the tequila ..."*

Oh my.

Now fascinated, I felt compelled to continue the work of putting all this together, so I did just that.

Not so long later, I had a whole page, but on one side of it, many of the words had been obliterated making them unreadable. What might that have been that he had to cross it out in addition to tearing up the pages?

On the good side, I could read this much: *"Also, there's the matter of our investment. That house means a lot to the fortune of many in my family. Not me so much, I've always done well, though of course I want it. But my brother and to some of our cousins, this investment is their chance to get ahead. It will be a while before we start making money from it, what with the renovations. Umberto says we can get eight studio apartments in there! That will bring a nice return once we can start renting them to short-term renters. I can't do anything to jeopardize that for them. They shouldn't lose out because a loser cousin, one involved with a cartel, no less, had something happen to him."*

I gazed into space. A memory came to me—my mother once mentioning that Camila and her husband, Sofia's parents, had bought into houses to renovate with family members with the purpose of doing short-term rentals.

The last sentence at the bottom of the page said "*If the police discover this, the whole project will fall apart.*"

When turned over, the first two paragraphs were crossed out. So, no way of knowing what it was he didn't want the police to discover. I felt more and more certain that it had something to do with that skeleton.

Below the crossed-out paragraphs, it said "*if only we'd known where his father had gotten the money! We'd never have allowed it. I never imagined that my uncle would accept money from a son in the cartel to invest into our project. If this comes out, they'll take all of the money in our investment account, not just that money.*"

What was I to do with all this information? Maybe it was time to fess up to Antonio. And Manuel.

Now being six a.m. there was no going back to sleep. Sounds from the waking city reached me despite the triple-pane windows. I found my way to the kitchen and filled the kettle.

And of course, my gaze traveled to the Gonzalez property. Whereas I'd once looked at the garden, since the murder, my eye was always drawn to the patio door, and a vision of Balaclava Man kept presenting itself to me. Sometimes with Pablo's face, sometimes with the faces of The Followers.

How could I figure out which of them had done it? And prove it?

CHAPTER 21

When I'd first arrived at the vigil, I'd invited the Gonzalezes to the *hacienda* for Sunday's *comida*, which was yesterday. They had accepted, with Alejandro and his wife agreeing to stay behind to host the vigil until the others returned.

At the time, my goal had been to get Pablo alone. But after hearing his phone conversation, and after my dream, I felt squeamish about talking to him. What could I say? *Oh, by the way, Pablo, I think you killed Aurelia? I saw you do it in a dream?*

Manuel had picked me up and before long, we'd pulled up to my parents' home.

The first thing I saw was my parents and Pablo talking on the verandah, him comforting Leonora, which conflicted with my suspicions of him.

Uncles, aunts, cousins, and their families meandered about everywhere while music played, the genre changing often to satisfy all generations, while meat on the grill scented the air.

In time, I managed to get close enough to Pablo while being far enough from the others to engage him in a more or less private conversation. I kept my feelings in check while mentioning that, while at the vigil, I'd meant to say that I'd seen someone who looked at lot like him with some men in El Jardin when I'd been on my way elsewhere, and had it been him?

My heart pounding, I tried to gauge his reaction. He had denied it, but had looked uncomfortable and extricated himself from our conversation as fast as he could, claiming to have to attend to his children, who'd gone to the playground on the side of my parents' house.

So, this morning, I woke up feeling jittery. One day closer to my wedding, and no closer to solving the murders, despite all that I knew.

Guilt sat itself right on top of the jitters because of the lies I'd told Antonio, or rather, the things I wasn't disclosing to him and Manuel ...

Why couldn't I, like a normal person, tell Antonio everything and let him do his job? Because I wanted it done and over with. So I could put all such happenings behind me. No more sleuthing. Forever. Even if he wanted to work faster, the man was busy with two other killings, and all that that involved. And a skeleton in a yard. And Ramon's death, too.

Once I got to the rooftop as usual, I was happy to see that no one had tried to break in overnight, the noises of Centro sounded normal, and the view—azure skies with a few wispy white clouds—was glorious. I could almost believe that none of the latest events had happened.

As I gazed at our famed Parroquia, Pablo and his reaction to our conversation at the *hacienda* came to mind.

On the spur of the moment, I decided to bring the Gonzalezes pastries to have with their morning coffee. I'd stop at my favorite bakery just around the corner on Pila Seca. Thoughts of the bakery's aroma, a blend of fresh bread, cinnamon, cumin, and coffee, made my mouth water. This scent often drew a crowd, sparking a friendly scramble for the few tables. It fostered a lively atmosphere. And if I left now, I'd beat the morning rush.

The pastries would be a good distraction to explain my visit to the Gonzalezes. Because something in me was saying that the answer I sought about Aurelia's murder was to be found in her house, so going there was necessary.

"Come, Dapperoo, mommy has to go to work."

As if he understood, he pulled himself up and out of the ray of sunshine in which he'd been basking, following me through the rooftop door, which I carefully locked after it closed with its usual loud clang. I stared at the door a moment, certain that I couldn't have missed this ritual the other day, yet Manuel and I had found it open ...

Dressing quickly, I chose a midi dress of my own design, tan, loose body, one sleeve, as well as a band around the round neckline, in the azure of our San Miguel skies, the other sleeve and the hem in a soft orange. On my feet went a pair of flat Tory Birch capri beaded strappy sandals with bubbly gold tone bead accents on slim leather straps.

I arrived at the Gonzalez home and rang the doorbell at the street door. A static crackle broke the morning silence before a male voice responded from within, its cautious tone floating through the intercom.

"¿*Bueno*?" Yes. The voice sounded tinny, but I recognized it.

"¿Alejandro?"

A moment passed as if he were going through a mental Rolodex, trying to figure out who was asking.

"¿Ah, Carli?"

"Sí. I brought pastries for your breakfast. And candies for the little ones. For later." The thought of their reaction made me smile.

"Bueno, entra. Ya conoces el camino." Come in, you know the way.

The gate buzzed and clicked open, granting me access to the well-manicured courtyard.

Just then, a FedEx truck pulled up to the curb, the driver jumped out, asked if I was going inside and when I said yes, pushed a flat envelope into my hands, then jumped back into his truck as if there was a fire behind him.

Looking down at it, I saw that it was addressed to Pablo Ortega. Without thinking, I shoved it deep into my tote. My heart hammered away, but with all my instincts telling me that its content had something to do with what was happening, what else could I do?

I made my way through the courtyard and to the house. The Gonzalez children, their children, Pablo, and Alejandro's wife, all welcomed me despite my arrival at the ungodly hour of eight-thirty in the morning.

No doubt the scent emanating from the bakery bags helped a little with that. They exclaimed over them, and it kept me from thinking of the large white envelope with the blue and dark orange logo I'd shoved in my bag.

What did it contain?

CHAPTER 22

M onday nights were for what I called *The Culling of the Clothes* in my shop.

It meant riffling through all the clothing racks with a critical eye, much like weeding a garden; no weeds allowed around the beautiful flowers made up of gorgeous vintage and other designer treasures. And no faded flowers allowed to remain.

The reputation of Carli's Secret Closet depended on its display of fresh-looking clothes, despite it being a consignment shop. With customers streaming in and out of the store throughout the day, this necessary task most often took place after Monday's closing time of six p.m. But, after doing some of it during lunch, I decided to leave the rest for tomorrow.

Tonight, Luna and I had work to do. I texted her and reminded her about it. Also, the FedEx envelope in my tote bag was burning holes in it and in my mind. There'd been no chance to look at it yet, as I'd left the Gonzalez home later than expected, and had needed to get to the shop. Which had been extra busy all day.

Manuel never expected to spend time with me on Mondays—he planned on me being at my shop. So I knew he wouldn't call for us to get together impromptu.

Luna couldn't have arrived a moment too soon. I'd wanted her with me when I tore the envelope open in case I ever needed to testify as to what I found in it. Sure, I was reaching, but one never knew.

She arrived with her usual fanfare, wearing an outfit in an explosion of colors, which no one else in the world could get away with wearing. Of course. And carrying a good bottle of Côtes du Rhône wine. She clutched the bottle of red to her chest, and pulled me into a hug with her other arm before we made our way to the second floor, and both flopped into my down-filled couch, an experience that felt like falling into a cloud—if clouds could hold humans, that is.

"Dap, my man!" She exclaimed as soon as Dap showed up, standing erect, checking out her vibe for whether she had a treat for him. She did not, and so headed to the kitchen to get one of mine. Meanwhile, she talked up a storm about our puzzle, which I'd just brought to the dining room.

She came back and sat next to me, ignoring Dap. Soon, he came by her and rubbed his face against her leg. Then, she happened to "notice" him, ha ha. She was funny, my Luna.

"Dapper! Your *mamá* tells me you've been a good boy. So ..." she reached into the top of her cleavage of all places!, and pulled out two salmon treats and presented them to him with a flourish. My eyes rolled of their own accord. Luna!

He sniffed at them a bit, put both in his mouth, and ran off toward the couch, but I seized him and put him in my bedroom instead, closing the door so he wouldn't go after the pages. He meowed pitifully a couple of times before calming himself and going silent.

The whole spectacle dazzled me to the brink of forgetting the FedEx envelope.

"Oh, Luna, guess what I got today?" I asked, as I took it from the coffee table and ripped it open.

Luna watched me with curiosity, waiting to see what I'd pull out of there.

One single sheet of typewritten paper slipped out. Luna and I looked at one another like deer caught in headlights, then we both leaned toward the letter, our heads touching as I read out loud, though, she could see it just as well.

Pablo, we've been trying to talk to you alone out of respect, but you are always with family. And you're not answering your phone. So, we were forced to send this letter.

El jefe won't wait much longer. You know what you have to do, and very soon.

We know where you and your pretty wife and your child live in Guanajuato, where her brother the big doctor lives in D.F. with his wife and his two children, and even where that other sister lives and works in Albuquerque. Yes, we have people there, too.

And, of course, we know where Santiago lives, and your parents ...

Don't make us do some terrible thing we have no desire to do.

We give you no more than 10 days to come up with it. All of it. Otherwise, you know what will happen.

That was all. No signature. I stared at it. Luna and I remained silent, she, looking as confused and surprised as I was. Even the city around us seemed to go quiet for a moment.

"Luna, this makes no sense. Who's Santiago? They're talking to Pablo, *si*? And clearly, they're bad men. Why do they say that they haven't been able to talk to him when I saw him with them in El Jardin?

"At least, I'm assuming this was sent by those followers of mine." Frowning, I closed my eyes trying to put all the pieces of everything happening into some sort of order that made sense.

"Unless he's got some doings with more than one set of bad guys ..." said Luna, her voice dreamy like.

We looked at one another and said it almost at the same time.

"Nah." Neither of us believed in coincidences, or in things with no explanation. The simplest explanation was often the right one. This meant that the men who'd been stalking me, coming to my shop, and meeting with Pablo had written this letter.

What didn't make sense was that they didn't seem to know they'd met with him. This thought twisted and turned in my head. I decided to think of something else, hoping that if I left it alone, an answer would come to me.

"Well, we can't do anything about it now. I need to think. Meanwhile ..."

I glanced at the dining room table and the puzzle.

Luna followed my gaze. "You're right. We should do what we can do right now." She got up from couch and stretched, yawning.

I extricated myself from the depths of the couch and followed her to the dining room.

We sat at the table and prepared to get going on the puzzle. There were still at least fifty loose pieces in all sorts of shapes and sizes.

"Should I open the window? It's a nice night. If you don't mind the noise?" Anticipating her response, I walked to the large window in the living room, tightening my ponytail on the way.

Luna shrugged and pursed her lips, which meant she didn't care either way.

I opened two of the window panels, letting in the night air, a slight breeze just moving the sheer curtains, but of course, also letting in the sound of traffic and other city noises, including firecrackers in the distance.

We got to work, one or the other of us getting up every now and again to go take a sip of our wine, which we'd left on the coffee table to avoid spilling any on our puzzle.

Each of us kept coming up with more ideas about what the FedEx letter could be referencing, what the threat might be, but it was no use.

After about an hour, Luna rose to stretch, her movements graceful. She looked like a modern-day Goddess version of a long-gone tribe, or at least a Hollywood version of it, her flowing caftan a riot of primary colors—red, purple, yellow, green, orange, and blue.

"What do you think? Enough for tonight?" She said, sounding tired, and yawning again.

I hesitated. We were so much closer, now just shy of four full pages and about twenty-five loose pieces, though these were the smaller ones, so it would be more tedious to find their place in this large puzzle of ours.

"Yeah ... maybe I'll do a little more." I said, gazing at all the paper strewn about the table. Firecrackers went off nearby and were quite loud. I went to the window and closed the panels.

"No, *chica*. It's eleven o'clock. We both need sleep." Luna looked at me with furrowed brows.

I sighed. "Okay ... you're right."

We put the puzzle away, but not before we'd read what we now had.

So far, six pages, but missing too many pieces, and they had too many crossed-out words to know for certain what it all said. The new information we got tonight seemed to be that someone had had too much tequila, but a piece was missing right before that, so we didn't know who.

And then, it said: "... *sometimes for weeks at a time. No one wanted to know what he did ... went and got himself lost in Belize or Brazil to escape the car ...* "

On the back of that same page near the top, it said "... *to my family ... what would happen?"* Then, farther down, we found this little gem: "*As I understand it, revenge killings often involve them killing the entire family and not just the one who wronged them!*"

Luna grabbed my arm as we read this part together.

"Oh my goodness, oh my goodness, Carli, what the heck??"

I couldn't answer her, transfixed on those words as I was.

The rest of both sides of this page had too many crossed-out words for us to put anything else together. This journal *must* be linked to the skeleton.

CHAPTER 23

The next day, I woke up with my head hurting a little. I'd had a second glass of wine on a nearly empty stomach, so no wonder. This case was taking me out of my usual self-care. That wouldn't do.

I sank deeper into my bed, hugging a pillow and pulling the down quilt over myself. Soon, Manuel would be joining me in this cocoon. A blush crept up my whole body at the thought, and my heart filled with love for him, for life, for my family, for the whole world!

And then, I remembered Aurelia. And the men following me. And the skeleton. And Pablo. In a huff, I pushed the comforter off, and sat up.

I reached to the foot of the bed and grabbed my robe—a refurbished vintage velvet beauty that belonged on a fifties' Hollywood movie set with its luscious deep teal stretch velvet, deep pockets, an attached waist tie, and three-quarter sleeves that ended just below the elbow in a wide pleated frill. They were called *peignoirs*, the French name for bathrobes, but now everyone just called them bathrobes, which was a shame. There's no romance, no artistic flair in "bathrobe."

As I went through my morning routine, all the discoveries I'd made last night swam in my head. I wondered whether to take the FedEx envelope back to the Gonzalez home. What could be my excuse? Would it not look suspicious if I returned today with more pastries?

But I couldn't go later when mourners arrived for the vigil. There would be people all over the house, and no opportunity for me to leave the envelope where it was most likely to be found: on the hall table.

Plus, there was the fact that to open it, I'd pulled the narrow strip of cardboard along its edge rather than steam it open, which would have been wiser. Pablo would know it had been tampered with.

And if I went over there now and he found the envelope either while I was there, or soon after, he'd know it was me, and that would open a whole hornet's nest.

I sighed, and started down to the kitchen to return my cup as the bells of Church of the Immaculate Conception, a bit farther away from the Parroquia, began to toll.

I stopped short on the staircase, getting an annoyed meow out of Dap, who'd been hot on my heels. I'd just thought of a way into the Gonzalez house without too much suspicion, and before mourners arrived.

I got dressed and threw a couple of treats into Dap's bowl before "abandoning" him once more for a full day. At least, that's what I thought he thought.

Just when I was about to open the front door to leave, I remembered the envelope, my reason for going in the first place, and tsk'd at myself, turned around, and went to retrieve it from the shelf I'd put it on in my closet, placing it deep in my tote bag, making sure the top of it didn't show.

The sun shone so beautifully, as usual, and the bluest of blue skies faced me as I turned my head to it. I breathed in my town, taking in the traffic sounds, the exhaust fumes, even, the noise of the church bells near and farther out, always there to tell us of the baptisms, funerals, high masses, and of course, ringing at every hour, except on Good Friday, out of the respect for the death of Jesus.

I walked to the corner, took a right, and turned right again, which placed me on the street behind mine.

Soon, Graciela buzzed me in, and I strolled through the court-yard toward the front door. I squared myself and reached for the doorbell, but the door opened and there stood ... Pablo.

"Pablo! *Hola*." I said, for some reason shocked to see him. But, of course, he was here. His wife was here, his child was here, his in-laws had lived here. Even if he might have killed one of them, since he hadn't been arrested for it, he still had every right.

"Carli. *¿Cómo estás?"* Was he looking at me speculatively?

"Bien, bien, Pablo. Gracias." It was so hard, but I smiled at him.

We shook hands and it took all I had in me to not then wipe my hand on my pants.

"Venir." Come.

He waved me in. Despite his friendly demeanor, one could not miss his strained smile, his anxious energy. What secrets did he have?

What had he meant during that phone call I'd heard? Should I just ask him? Of course not. What would that look like?

Plus, would that not put me in more danger than I already was? Right now, to me, he was Balaclava Man. And Balaclava Man was a killer. The only doubt that he wasn't him was that phone call ...

The sound of young children laughing reached me from the kitchen in the back and, smiling at Pablo again, I followed it.

The families had gathered around the large kitchen table which held various platters and bowls of breakfast foods. Scrambled eggs, tortillas, bacon and sausages, a large bowl of beans. It made me hungry, but I wouldn't be eating any of it.

"Hola a todos!" I called out cheerily. Hi everyone.

A chorus of "*Buenas dias*, Carli!" rang out, making me smile despite the situation in which we all found ourselves.

"Come, Carli. Are you hungry? Will you join us?"

"No, Graciela, *gracias*, I came to make you and Leonora an offer," I said, glancing at Leonora, too, giving both my best smile, as the FedEx envelope felt like a live thing in my bag, one that could pop out at any moment and make itself known.

"Oh?" Said Leonora, stopping with a cup of coffee halfway to her mouth.

The young ones all stared at me, too, curious.

"Well, I was thinking that you might like some help with mourning clothes, especially for the *velorio,* but also for the vigil?" The funeral.

"Ah ..." exclaimed Leonora, turning to gaze at her sister.

Alejandro and Pablo looked at their wives, then at one another, incomprehension on their faces. To them, any old black dress would do.

They didn't understand the importance to a woman of looking good for their *mamá* and *papá* even though they'd gone to "the other side." It was one more way to honor them.

"I have a shop full of clothes. We can find great pieces. You will both look beautiful for your parents."

While I spoke, I'd sat at a vacant chair at the table. Now, tears came to my eyes. Theirs too.

At first, they remained silent. Then, they both got up and came to me. I stood, too, and we hugged.

One of the children brought a huge bucket of Legos and dumped them on the floor of the living room ... in a spot in full view of the entire entry hallway. A sigh escaped me, and I barely kept to myself the grunt that followed.

No way could I leave the envelope now without being detected. And, anyway, I hadn't solved the problem of the envelope having been opened already.

We arranged for the sisters to meet me at Carli's Secret Closet in an hour or so. I left, shooting a look of longing at the hall table with the many family photos on its surface, wishing I could put the FedEx envelope on it, but not while in full view of the children. And, anyway, I hadn't solved the little problem of the envelope having already been opened.

I could think of no way to return it without creating suspicion. I'd have to keep it ...

But, who should I see as soon as I stepped foot on the pavement just outside the house?

CHAPTER 24

The Gonzalez sisters arrived at my boutique two hours after I'd left their house. By then, I'd managed to put aside several dresses for them to choose from. For Graciela, the more conservative one, a Theory Varetta admiral crepe sheath dress for the funeral day, and an Isabelle funnel neck dress with dolman sleeves to wear in the days before and after. Also, a black St-John mixed rib button skirt, and several black tops, so she could interchange them each day she wore the skirt, including a real find, a black St-John boucle pocket cardigan, a perfect match for the skirt. This would take her through her time here.

For Leonora, who liked to dress a little flashier, a Tuckernuck black guipure lace daphne dress. Also for her, a Lafayette 148 twisted front dress, and a Karen Kane sheer blouson sleeve dress, a Vince long paneled cutwork slip skirt, and various black tops to interchange.

We also chose hats and discreet jewelry for them. Now, they just needed their own shoes and handbags, which they said they'd brought with them from home, in black, and in triplicate, even.

Though I hadn't accomplished my goal behind going to them and making this offer, I liked being able to help them at this terrible time. My consigners would need to be paid, of course, but I'd worry about the money later.

Still, the whole day, despite all these goings-on, The Followers never left my mind.

They'd been sitting in the front seat of a dark grey SUV with the engine running, right across the street from the Gonzalez house when I'd come out. Both had turned toward me, not bothering to hide, not caring that I knew they were following me. How had they known I'd be here, though?

On the spur of the moment, after taking a huge breath, that is, having had enough of them, I walked up to their car and knocked on the driver's side window even though I knew he could see me, standing right there in front of his car.

The driver, the one who'd bought the gift certificate from my shop, rolled down his window.

"Are you looking for me?" I asked, feeling brazen.

The look on his face showed surprise at my boldness. It had taken him a moment, but I'd kept staring, and shifty-eyed, he replied.

"We are not here for you, *señorita*."

I leaned down so both men could see my face, then raised my eyebrows while keeping my eyes on the driver. The one in the passenger seat turned from me and looked out his window.

*"Señorita Cano, no te molestes con esto, "*the driver said. Don't bother yourself with this.

"Well, I want to know what's going on. You are coming to my shop all the time, yes, I see you both walking by it. And now you are here."

"Ah, *señorita,* you will only cause trouble for yourself with your behavior!"

I stared at him, nothing coming to mind to say in response. Until ...

"And I think you came into my house. *Sí?*"

His eyes sparked with a cold twinkle that pierced through me. He dared harass me in my own town, trouble adult children grieving their parents, neighbors I had cared about? Even having possibly killed one of those parents? And laugh about it? No!

"You should know, I saw you coming out of the Gonzalez home on the morning of *la Señorita* Gonzalez's death."

He sat, frozen in place, his expression blank, a true professional. Criminal, that is. Give nothing away.

What had I just done? It took everything in me to stop myself from clapping a hand over my mouth. If they'd only been following me before, what would they do now that I'd brought this out in the open? Obviously, they'd known I'd seen the man come out of Aurelia's house, or they wouldn't have been following me.

A car went by, driving much too fast on the narrow street, a popular song by our very own Mexican boy who-made-good-as-a-rapper, C-Kan, blasting from the radio.

The driver and I turned to look at it, distracted.

As soon as the car passed, we both once again turned to one another. I liked the advantage of me standing while he sat, but now, after looking up and down the street, he opened the car door and stepped out. Still, my height of at least six inches above him, including the Jimmy Choo Diosa platform wedge sandals on my feet, left him at a disadvantage, due to his shorter height of about five foot five or so.

My body shaking, heart hammering away, I took a modified Jiu-Jitsu fighting stance so he wouldn't know I was preparing myself in case he attacked—feet shoulder-width apart, right foot forward, my left leg flexed, weight distributed between the balls of my feet, hips square, my chest up, arms at my side, and hands open.

Despite the chaos of fear in my body, I held my head high and forced my eyes to remain on his.

Our height difference didn't seem to intimidate him at all. He smirked, which angered me even more. I was a joke to him.

"Señorita Cano, Carli, we are just ... "

I interrupted him. *"Señorita* Cano, *por favor."* Please.

Saying nothing, I gave him my fiercest look. He returned it with hatred spewing from his eyes, and this quick transformation unsettled me.

"We want nothing with you, but to have you stay out of our business." He crossed his arms, taking on his own fighting stance, frowning.

"I'm not in your business." I took a deep breath, doing my best to slow down my heart rate despite the tense situation. Another car crept by, but ignored us.

Now, the Follower facing me looked downright mean, a sharp glint in his eyes, a hard look. He'd grown impatient with me, I could see.

"Calling the police just because our friend was leaving the house of another friend *is* being in our business." A nasty smirk took over his whole face.

His voice never rose above a whisper. I cursed myself for not turning on the voice recorder on my phone, but how was I to know that he'd be here?

"Ah? Was it you that I saw, *Señor* ... "

He waved my unasked question for his name away.

"No es importante." It's not important.

"Ah, no? And what about my dead neighbor? Is that not important? And her husband, was that you, too?" Only the help of God kept me from foaming at the mouth, such was my anger.

He laughed. Laughed at me!

I persisted. "It was you coming out of the house that morning. *Sí?*" I stood, arms crossed, my face on fire from the anger that consumed me.

He remained silent for several beats, face blank. Then, he surprised me with what he said next.

"That family," he nodded his head in the direction of the Gonzalez house, "they have big *problema, señorita, problema muy grande."* A very big problem.

He re-crossed his arms and stared at me, all efforts to look like a normal man—one not in a *cartel* and in the habit of killing people—discarded. The man standing in front of me was the real thing, a real mean one.

I pulled my arms closer to my body to stop the trembling that had started up as I watched his transformation into the thug he was.

"What problems?" I still managed to ask.

He shrugged.

"The problem of many families, *por supuesto*—of course—money. They want money on the spot, and they are not thinking to pay it back. Well, my *jefe*, he likes to be paid back." He spoke with conviction.

Nodding again in the direction of the Gonzalez house, he continued.

"One of them owes my *jefe*, and now someone in his family just wants to help."

Surprised he admitted something like this, yet not understanding what he meant, I stared at the ground in front of me, while keeping an eye on him, of course, trying to work it out.

A small white car drove by, engine rumbling, all windows open, and the lone man in it glanced at us, then looked away. I kept it in my peripheral vision, wondering if the other Follower still sitting in the car had called for backup. And now I'd be caught and kidnapped by several men. I could take one on with my Jiu Jitsu skills, but two or more?

"Who? Who owes your *jefe* money?" I pushed.

"They're your *amigos*, you figure it out." He shrugged with his left shoulder only, his eyes darting to the Gonzalez house for a split second. "Just be sure to tell him that he better settle his debts as soon as possible, or ... you know ..." He raised his eyebrows while staring into my eyes to see if I understood.

"You are *usurero?*" Loan shark.

He chuckled, then smiled the smile of a man who believes he has the upper hand.

Had Pablo's business been in trouble, and he'd borrowed money from bad men? And what did this Follower mean by saying "someone in that person's family just wants to help?"

If it was Pablo who had borrowed money, and it seemed that it must be, considering that FedEx letter, he could have asked Ramon for money. As their daughter's husband, they'd have helped him out to avoid the scandal of him going to a *usurero*, something a respectable family like the Gonzalezes would not stoop to unless desperate.

And who in the family was trying to help him?

As I'd tried to figure all this out, he'd spoken up.

"If you get in the way of this going well, *Señorita* Cano, you will be in the cross hairs of my *jefe*, and those of us who work for him. *Comprend*e?" Understand.

His face was hard now. Social hour was over.

CHAPTER 25

T wo nights from tomorrow, I'd spend my last night as a single woman in my childhood bedroom. This coming Saturday, I would be sharing a bed with Manuel, in a luxurious suite overlooking a large vineyard, just a few miles from here. The thought made me blush.

But. This puzzle had to be ... *puzzled* out before then. No dead bodies were to accompany me to the altar even if only in my mind.

My plan had been to take the three remaining days before my big day to just relax, to take care of any last preparations, though those were in our mothers' hands. They didn't even want *me*, the bride, "in the way"!

With their excellent taste in everything, I felt no qualms about this at all. Besides, being married to Manuel was all that counted for me. The color of the napkins or of the flowers on all the tables that were being set up now on the grounds right in front of my parents' house at our hacienda mattered not at all to me. Luna found this strange, considering my obsession with style when it came to clothes. I shrugged it off.

My gown, and my man were all I wanted control over. Manuel. If he only knew what I'd gotten myself into ...

For the next few days, Esme and Sofia would manage the shop for me. My only involvement would be to take their calls and answer questions if need be. My time was my own. We would be closed from Friday until the following Tuesday so that no complications could arise to distract me from my nuptials and our mini honeymoon of three nights at the winery.

So, time to step up my inquiries into the death of a certain Aurelia Gonzalez, neighbor, friend, and customer. And to solve it. Also time to figure out about that skeleton in Eduardo's yard.

No more mayhem here!

After my confrontation with The Followers, though I'd worked at my shop, I hadn't been able to erase them from my mind. I recalled what the one outside the car had said. *If you get in the way of this going well, Señorita Cano, you will be in the cross hairs of my jefe, and those of us who work for him. Comprende?*

He'd then gotten in the car and peeled off, giving me a friendly wave ... and a smile. The nerve!

The fear I'd felt then returned, like a strong wave rising from out of nowhere and hitting the beach hard, threatening to knock me down. What was I doing getting involved in all this?

Yet, I couldn't ignore the compulsion to move forward. I had three days! No, just two full ones!

Manuel wouldn't be around me much until the wedding. We'd agreed that except for him coming to check that my house—soon, our house—was secure at night, we would just see one another at the altar.

I already missed him and couldn't wait until we could be together any time we wanted without the constraints of living apart and having to follow tradition. In theory, I loved tradition. In practice, not so much when it kept me from seeing the love of my life.

Now, I needed a plan. I headed to the roof with Dap, where we sat companionably, me, thinking, he, basking in the sun, but keeping a close eye on me as if he sensed my determination to get to the bottom of these murders. As if he wondered why I felt compelled to do it.

How would my Dapper be once Manuel lived here full time? I wondered. He liked Manuel who slipped him treats behind my back, Dap acting as if this wasn't happening, coming to me for treats as usual. They thought I didn't know. Ah. It dawned on me that I was about to start sharing my home with two traitors.

I continued to sit and stare into space, at the spires of the Parroquia, at the roofs of all the other buildings with their black *tinacos*—water tanks—as if the answers I needed hid in there.

A thought began to form in my head, but before it could materialize, roof dogs began yelping, something I usually overlooked.

Today, however, The Followers, Pablo, and Balaclava Man prominent in my mind, I jerked, sitting straight up. Perked my ears. Dap stood, no doubt catching my vibe. We listened for a moment, but the dogs settled, and I decided we should go back inside and sit on the couch instead so we could plan my next move with fewer distractions.

I sank into the couch, closed my eyes, and allowed my mind to meander back to my neighbors' home. What was it that nagged at me? What might I have seen or felt without realizing it?

My head shook of its own accord. I still felt that the house held a clue for me.

Tears welled up in my eyes. Such a nice family. To have this happen to them ...

I had to fix it. Just had to. A deep sigh escaped me. I couldn't forget the main events to take place before my actual nuptials, such as the day before that would be spent at my friend Ana's spa getting massages and facials with Mamá, Luna, and Amy, and then, a leisurely *comida*.

Our dresses were ready, my wedding gown now on a mannequin in my childhood bedroom at the *hacienda*, Luna's and Amy's hanging in their respective closets. My cousins acting as bridesmaids were also in possession of their dresses. We were all meeting at the church three hours before the wedding, to put the finishing touches on our makeup and for the train to be attached to my dress. The church was the only place I'd be wearing it. Already, my mind was working on how to repurpose it.

But before all that, murders had to be solved. My mind returned to Pablo. And The Followers.

I forced myself to breathe. Deeply in, deeply out. This was no time for an anxiety attack.

CHAPTER 26

From my position on the couch, my eyes traveled to the dining room table where the pieces of Eduardo's journal, now under a tablecloth to save them from Dap, distracted me.

Carefully, I removed the cloth, and almost immediately saw where a piece would fit perfectly on a nearly completed page, and placed it there. Then, another. Before long, I managed to put together a whole page!

Chills traveled up and down my spine as it began to look as if these pages held the answer to how that skeleton had ended up in Eduardo's garden. At the same time, a likely scenario began to take shape in my head.

What seemed like hours after I'd begun to work on the journal, I lifted my eyes, distracted by a loud and insistent car horn right in front of my house. I stretched and decided to see what all the ruckus, loud by even San Miguel standards, was about.

The plan had been for Luna and me to finish as much of the puzzle as possible this evening, to hopefully get it all done, but I'd done quite a bit this morning.

I swept away thoughts of how to give all this to Antonio without him exploding. Could I do it anonymously?

Through my living room window, I saw a car trying to get by a delivery van, parked, San Miguel style, right in the middle of the street, blocking traffic. I sighed. The delivery driver seemed nowhere in sight.

Could I solve all these things in just a couple of days? Doubt crept up in me like a fast-growing vine. Still, A Cano did not give up so easily.

My great-great-grandfather and his brother had encountered worse things as they built our hacienda. I could do this. And if I couldn't, then so be it. With this solved or not, no more sleuthing for me, in any case.

My mind believed I'd walk away from any future mysteries. Now, if I could only get my heart to follow.

Last night, at a loss as to where to start regarding Pablo, I'd felt compelled to search for him online.

I'd searched Pablo's name on its own, but not much had come up. I'd searched his name with Leonora's, looked at Facebook, Instagram, and, nothing. Too tired to continue, I'd given up and gone to bed.

But now, I had an idea for a new search and wondered why I hadn't thought of it before. If it didn't pan out, I'd ask Luna to do it; she was the hacker, after all. Even if this didn't require hacking, at least not right now, she might be faster at finding answers.

I booted up my laptop and brought it to the dining room table. Before beginning my search, I took a sip of tea, stretched my fingers, and admired my engagement ring. Now, I was ready.

In the search bar, I entered "Pablo+Ortega+tourist+shop owner+Guanajuato." A few results came up, including a listing on an official website showing the names of three shops under Pablo's name, but saying nothing more beyond that and the locations of the shops.

In a bit of a daze, thinking, I kept scrolling and on Page 2 of the results, I came across an article written by none other than Jorge Garcia, my *papá's* brother's son! Yes, I seemed to have more cousins, and second, and third and fourth cousins than most people I knew outside my family.

It often came in very handy. For instance, this particular cousin had worked as an investigative journalist in Mexico City for several years, but had returned to San Miguel to live just two months ago.

Dap came to twirl himself around my legs, meowing like a starved creature so that I'd give him a treat. So he could forgive me. For being so rude as to disturb him off my lap when I'd gotten up from the sofa. I grunted. There'd be no peace until I complied with my spoiled cat's demand.

"Happy, Dapperoo?" I asked as he delicately took the treat from my fingers as though doing me a favor. I chuckled and returned my attention to my laptop.

The article I'd found was about illegal gambling in Mexico. Why had that come up in my search for Pablo, I wondered, my eyebrows knitting. In it, Jorge did an analysis of the people who gamble illegally, their motives and reason. He wrote about a raid in Guanajuato. I continued to scan the article, wondering what it had to do with Pablo, why it had appeared when I searched his name.

Then, I gasped at this next thing: "among others, a manufacturer of clothing from Monterey, the owner of several restaurants both in San Miguel de Allende and Guanajuato, *and a tourist shop owner, also from Guanajuato.*" The article hadn't come up because of his name, but because of this.

In all, seven men were arrested when police raided the illegal card game taking place in a room at the back of one of the restaurant owner's locations in Guanajuato.

I next searched "Pablo Ortega+arrest+gambling," which brought up something on a website three pages down.

And there it was. *Pablo Ortega arrested six months ago during the police raid of an illegal card game in Guanajuato.*

CHAPTER 27

I t seemed that Pablo had gotten himself arrested right around the time I'd been busy figuring out another murder. So, I'd missed seeing this article. Even if Ramon and Aurelia Gonzalez had known about the arrest, shame would have kept them from telling anyone about it. Did Leonora know? I wondered.

It had to be him. How many Pablo Ortega who owned tourist shops in Guanajuato could there be? Did Antonio already know about it?

After giving it some thought, it seemed that Jorge was the best place to start looking into this since I had no other leads.

Jorge sometimes went to El Café in the afternoons around three, and it was now two-thirty. I decided to go without contacting him first. Let him think it was a coincidence me running into him there. I didn't want questions about why I was asking questions.

I got dressed in a casual outfit—black leggings and a beautiful, black sleeveless Alberta Ferretti tunic. On my feet, my favorite flats, a pair of black Dolce&Gabbana leather sandals, and a perfect match to it all, a Dolce&Gabbana printed flower tote in their papaver color.

Smiling despite all the murder mysteries swimming in my head, I was at the threshold of the door when I remembered I had a hat for Graciela for the funeral. It fit in my tote, and I could drop it off after meeting with Jorge. *If* I got to meet with Jorge, I clarified in my mind.

As I walked toward the heart of Centro and what I hoped would be a productive "chance" meeting, I breathed in my town. No matter what went on in my life, I felt grateful for the charm of the buildings and of the people all around me, the sound of church bells, the smell of food that often made my mouth water as I walked by food carts.

I saw Jorge as soon as I entered El Café, sitting at a high table on the opposite side of the order counter. Perfect!

He happened to look up, and our eyes met. His face broke out in a grin, and he opened his arms wide in greeting. I pointed to the order counter and mouthed that I'd be right there. He stood and came to me instead.

"*¿Cómo te va, vato?*" How are you, dude. I gave him a hug.

"Carli! *Ven, mi prima favorita!*" Come, my favorite cousin. He took me into a warm embrace. I fell into it, relishing the moment of comfort it brought me.

"Jorge, I missed you! It's about time you came home."

"So says the woman who lived in New York City for four years, taking her sweet time coming back. Whereas I," he said, stretching himself to his full height while pointing at his chest with his thumb, "was only a four-hour drive away. Or close to it."

We both laughed.

"Are you ready for your wedding?" Curiosity showed on his face. He must have wondered why I was here instead of at the hacienda preparing.

"*Sí*. Mamá is doing everything. Won't let me lift a finger. I did my dress and chose the bouquet, oh, and the groom, but nothing else."

He burst out laughing, and I joined him.

"*Por supuesto*!" He said. "*Por supuesto*." He knew my mother well and wasn't surprised. Of course.

"Better for me, you know. I just want to wear the dress, and finally be married to Manuel, that's all. We could have done it right here."

He looked around the coffee shop and smirked. He knew this wasn't true, but he humored me. "*Pues, por qué no?*" Well, why not.

By then, I was at the head of the line and ordered matcha and a pastry, hunger gnawing at me.

"*¿Hora del postre?*" He asked with a smile. Dessert time.

I nodded and we walked to his table where I made myself comfortable. We caught up on family as the usual bustle of the coffee shop surrounded us.

Once my drink was ready, I finally got to the part of the conversation I'd wanted to have from the moment I'd left my house.

"So, what's the most interesting article you wrote lately?"

"Oh, so many. Let's see ..." He stopped to take a sip of coffee while thinking. I seized the moment.

"Anything to do with anyone here in town?" I held my breath. Would the question make him suspicious?

He shook his head as he put down his coffee cup. But then he shifted, and his eyes lit up.

"Wait! Not from San Miguel, but I wrote an article on illegal gambling and how some people of means get caught up in it. One of the people mentioned is married to a woman from here, but they live in Guanajuato."

Ah. There. I'd made no real plans about what I'd ask him. Now, I wondered. Should I disclose that I knew the "one of them"? If so, he'd know I came with the intent to ask about Pablo. And I couldn't have that, not yet.

So, instead, I went with surprise. "*¿Realmente?*" Really.

"Sí, a Pablo Ortega. Married to a Gonzalez from here." There, out in the open. And *he*'d told *me*, not the other way around. Now, I could pretend I just wanted to gossip.

"Gonzalez? Pablo? Jorge, I know those people! They're my neighbors, the Gonzalezes."

Thank goodness for the two acting classes I'd taken for fun during college. Still, he stared at me, his eyes crinkling ever so much in the corners.

I made myself look sad, and it wasn't all acting.

"Jorge, the Gonzalez family ... do you know what happened to them? Just this past week?"

Someone with a large dog walked by us then, setting off a smaller dog's furious barking. The entire shop turned to look, and even the milk steamer's hiss stopped. The brief commotion ended with the large dog's owner leading him outside to the patio, but it distracted us.

Now, Jorge looked back my way, lifting his chin in my direction, as a way to ask me to tell him more.

"Well, the husband, Ram ... well, first of all, they're, they were, I mean, my neighbors. From behind my house."

"Oh, very close neighbors, then." He was curious now, looking at me with speculation.

"And, well, last Wednesday night, Ramon dropped dead in front of me in El Jardin."

Jorge coughed from the sip of coffee he'd been taking while I said this. He looked at me in surprise, shaking his head, a smile playing along his lips. "How do these things happen around you, Carli?"

"I went to El Jardin to meet up with Manuel, not Ramon Gonzalez! He just dropped at my feet. Antonio thinks it's either a heart attack or a poison given to him before he got to the square." I took a deep breath. "But that's not all," I added.

His forehead lifted and he tilted his chin up in my direction, his way to asking me to proceed, curiosity shining from his eyes.

"The next morning, his wife was found dead in her bed."

"*¿Mande?*" What. He asked. Someone else might have been shocked, but after writing about crime for years, this news only caused an uptick in interest to dawn in Jorge's eyes.

"Sí, I saw the murderer come out of their house ..." I watched his reaction.

He didn't respond, but his eyes were on me puzzling out something.

To continue without suspicion, I decided I should take the conversation in a different direction for a few minutes. Just then, a distraction presented itself in the person of my friend, Amy, who placed her hand on my shoulder.

"Amy! You're back!"

"Carli! Yes, I am!" She responded, her voice filled with warmth.

We laughed.

"So, your dress is ready, right?" I asked, leaning forward with anticipation.

"Of course, my darling. Can't wait for your big day! That's why we're here. Otherwise, we'd still be in Dallas with Douglas schmoozing people for his latest project."

She glanced at Jorge, curious, and I introduced them.

"Mucho gusto," he said, extending his hand toward Amy with a polite smile. She took it into her own, her expression open and friendly. Nice to meet you.

"So, Jorge and I are just catching up. Would you like to join us?" I asked, fingers crossed that she'd decline. That would end the conversation I wanted to have.

"Nah. I have an appointment at the hairdresser. Color and cut." She brushed a strand of hair behind her ear. "And don't worry. My hairdresser said she'll fluff it up on Saturday." She nodded, her tone reassuring.

"Oh, no need. Ana will be at the church for last-minute make-up and hair."

"Ooh, perfect, you're doin' this thing right, girl. Okay, gotta go, I'm running a teeny-weeny bit late." She winked at me.

I stood and gave her a quick hug and cheek kisses.

"Jorge, *mucho gusto*. Guess I'll see you at the wedding?" She said.

He stood, too, and they exchanged cheek kisses.

"Of course! It was very nice to meet you, too, Amy."

After she left, I asked a question that would bring Jorge and I back to talking about Pablo.

"Jorge, is it true that the cartels kill people who don't pay back their gambling debts?" I picked up my tea and drank, acting casual, as if his answer wasn't all that important to me, as if I were just a tad curious.

He looked somber, his eyes on me, looking unsure of what to say, or hesitant to say it.

The answer came, but not until he first glanced around for prying ears. "Yes." He pauses. "Yes, they do." He crossed his arms.

"How? Why?" I leaned toward him, scooting closer to the edge of the high stool.

"Well, they can't have people borrowing and not paying back with no consequences. Then, everyone would borrow from them and not bother to pay back."

I nodded at that.

"Where they go overboard and what makes it sometimes impossible to pay them all back is how they play the game of lending."

"Oh?" I did my best to continue to only appear mildly curious.

The sounds of the shop fell away. I found myself in a bubble of just Jorge and me, listening to the awful thing he told me.

"It isn't just gambling, Carli. It's loan sharks, too. If you'd read the follow-up articles to that one I wrote on gambling, you'd know that they operate under what's known as the *gota a gota* method—drop-by-drop—of lending money. They offer loans, and not just to gamblers. To shop owners, too."

He stared at me, letting it sink in. Like dominoes, clackety clack, which as how my brain often came to conclusions, I realized what he was telling me.

"Wait, you mean, Pab ..."

He nodded his head yes.

I sucked in a breath. "So, what happens when they lend the money?"

"First, right from the beginning the interest rate is high. Twenty percent." He cleared his throat and took a sip of water. "They go after small business owners in trouble, the ones a bank is not likely to lend money to. And street vendors who want to expand. Or anyone else who comes to them. But that's not the worst part."

"What do you mean?" My hands tightened into fists.

"Well, a few weeks after they give out the loan, within a month, the interest rate goes up to fifty percent ..." He watched me, gaging my reaction. "They threaten those who don't pay. If that doesn't work, they rob and sometimes even attack them. Regrettably, in some cases, police are involved in the scheme. So these people can't go to the police. Because, too often, that's when they disappear."

He shrugged, shaking his head. "It's a bad, bad, situation, Carli."

My mouth dropped open in an O.

"Oh, my ... this is awful!"

He said nothing, his lips in a tight smile, nodding.

I didn't want him to know that I felt certain Pablo had used these lenders. But it explained The Followers outside his house, the letter, and the meeting in El Jardin.

Pablo owed them, or rather their *jefe*. And it had to do with his arrest for gambling, no doubt. He must have lost at that game, and was arrested before whoever ran the game could collect from him. It must also mean that this same person hadn't paid the protection money, hence the police showing up and making arrests. What a mess.

And somehow, Aurelia's death was wrapped up in all of this.

CHAPTER 28

I left Jorge with promises to meet his new girlfriend at the reception, but told him he'd have to find me in the huge crowd that would be at the hacienda on that day.

"It'll be easier for you; you can just look for the one *chica* in a long white dress. I'll be with a very handsome man wearing a tuxedo." I smiled at him warmly.

He chuckled as he stood to hug me, and gave me a peck on each cheek.

I walked to the Gonzalez home to give Leonora the hat I'd brought to give to her, my mind in a whirl about Pablo, and gambling, and debts to a cartel.

Even though I was gathering good information, it felt as if my investigation was moving at a snail's pace. I had to be at Ana's spa tomorrow at 2:00 p.m. with everyone for my facial, massage, and manicure and pedicure appointments. No investigation could go on from that moment on.

Suddenly, my phone dinged and vibrated. A text from Manuel.

> Hola, mi amor. Just wanted to say I love you.

My heart melted when I saw this, and continued to melt as I replied.

> love you even more. Can't believe you'll be my husband on Saturday. Someone pinch me!

He replied with a series of laughing emojis, and

> believe it!

Somehow, he seemed to always reach out when I needed a boost the most. It didn't erase the guilt I felt for keeping things from him ...

At least, it would all be over soon. I felt sure of it.

As soon as I turned the corner onto the street of the Gonzalez home, I noticed a man just leaving it. He was headed in the opposite direction, so he didn't see me. Pablo. No.

I squinted, examined his clothes. He wore a long sleeved light blue shirt with no pattern on it, at least, not on the back. From this distance, wearing that outfit, it could be either Pablo or The Followers. Their bodies were so similar, same height, little difference in weight.

Instinct told me to follow whoever this was. And so I did, hoping no one from my neighbor's household saw me walk past.

As soon as I got to the main artery, Zacateros, there were enough pedestrians I could blend into that he shouldn't catch me following him. Cars drove by a little faster than on other streets, music playing loudly from some of them.

I took down my ponytail and put on the hat meant for Leonora, hoping it would be enough to keep him from recognizing me if he glanced back and saw me.

He never turned around, though, so it didn't seem he feared being followed.

When Zacateros ended and Ancha de San Antonio started, he continued toward the Institute Allende, our famous art school, and stopped walking when he was right across from it.

Then, my target (*listen to me, thinking like an operative of some sort!*) paused to look both ways. For a moment, I was afraid he'd spotted me, but instead, he simply crossed the street, dodging a couple of cars. Once on the other side, he kept walking past the Institute in the same direction he'd been going. Making sure he wasn't looking at me, I put the hat back in my tote and pulled out a colorful scarf and wrapped it around my neck.

I crossed the street, too, running for a few steps to avoid a car that had decided to speed up, and continued my pursuit. He turned left onto Calle El Cardo and then right, next to a small café, onto a street that led to a less savory part of this neighborhood. There were now fewer people around, giving him a better opportunity to catch me. My heart rate increased.

The air was thick with the aroma of frying churros and the faint scent of exhaust fumes. The sun beat down on my back, making me perspire.

Then, up ahead, about three buildings past the café, I saw courtyard doors wide open and with colorful signage, and billowing kites in blue, green, red, orange, and yellow hanging from the left and right of the top of the door frame. There must be at least one shop in that building. I could go in if need be. The now gritty texture of the cobblestone street beneath my feet made me more cautious with each step I took.

The man turned right just past the courtyard. From my distance, I couldn't see clearly, but it wasn't a street he turned onto; there was no true intersection, and cars were parked tightly on both sides. More than likely a *callejón*. Alley.

Once I reached the doorway with all the flags, I entered what I'd thought of as a courtyard, but turned out to be a shop, a wide space with several rows of shelves holding pottery of all sizes and shapes. I pretended to browse. A shop girl called out a greeting to me from behind a register counter and I returned it.

Her gaze went back to her phone to which she was tethered by a headset, with only one earbud in her ear. The smell of incense filled the air, and it seemed cooler than outside, giving me some relief from the heat.

I walked deeper into the shop, unsure about what to do next. As I got closer to the back, I could hear voices, men's voices. They sounded muffled, but I could make out angry tones. My skin prickled with apprehension.

Had he gone into a back room in this building? No. Because why would I be able to hear them from behind a wall?

Then, I looked up. Halfway up a fifteen-foot-high wall on my left were two narrow and rectangular windows, clerestory style. Wide open windows ...

I recognized the voice of The Follower who'd threatened me outside the Gonzalezes'. All the voices were clearer now, and I even felt their tension and frustration.

Fumbling, I discreetly reached inside my tote for my phone. Looking at it, I clicked on the recording app, holding the phone as if I were engaged with it in some other way. With no music playing in the store, the recorder should pick up the conversation.

I said a silent prayer that the shop clerk would continue to be more interested in her own phone than in me. Since I'd been in this aisle for several minutes already, she might feel compelled to come check on me. But as soon as I engaged the recording app, a notification on my phone showed that it couldn't be used because I didn't have enough battery life left. Frustrated, I shoved the phone back into my tote.

With ears wide open, hanging on their every word, I pretended to be interested in the pottery on the shelves. The smooth, cool ceramic felt soothing in my hands as I picked one up, then put it down, all to keep the shopgirl from getting suspicious.

I could now hear four distinct voices, each carrying a unique timbre that echoed through the open windows. The Follower I knew, his voice low and menacing; another voice I didn't recognize, higher pitched and more nasal; one that definitely sounded like Pablo's, but I couldn't be certain; and one that sent shivers down my spine, aggressive and barking orders in a harsh tone.

My heart knocked around my chest hard and loud, its rapid beats reverberating in my ears as I struggled to keep my breathing steady. The intensity of my anxiety made my palms clammy, and a bead of sweat trickled down my temple.

I strained to make out what they said over the pounding of my heart and as the ceiling fan above me began to hum louder.

Still, I caught enough of their conversation that the scope of their sinister activities began to emerge.

And what I heard froze the blood in my veins.

CHAPTER 29

T he man with the aggressive voice spoke Aurelia's name, his words cutting through the warm, stagnant air. The general rustle of the men moving about provided a backdrop to their conversation and to my eavesdropping.

"This needs to move faster. The *jefe* is tired of waiting." He cleared his throat.

"Does he know?" Another asked, but I couldn't tell who had spoken, or who they meant by "he." And "know" what?

Their voices intertwined like various notes in a song, which made it challenging to pinpoint a single speaker.

"When will he have the money?" Said the heavy, angry voice.

"No se." I heard a heavy sigh. I don't know.

It was said in a low voice, the speaker sounding despondent, his voice just audible over the fast beats of my heart, as I tried to remain still.

"Well, when do you plan to find out?" Asked the same voice. He sounded arrogant, angry, demanding, his words punctuated by the shuffling of his shoes on gravel, giving the impression of a bull in a ring preparing to skewer the *matador*.

No one replied, the atmosphere around them heavy, something I could feel despite there being a wall between us.

"One more week and that's it. We need confirmation of the *exact* date of the payment. *Pronto, sí?*" Quickly.

"Por supuesto." Said the despondent voice, sounding meek, in that way of someone who knows he's beat. Of course.

The aggressive one lowered his voice. "Otherwise, you know he won't be in this world much longer ..." He paused. "The *jefe* doesn't stand for being cheated of money that's rightfully his. And it's more than a million pesos. *Sabes?*" You know.

"Por supuesto." The despondent one repeated.

I heard a match being struck and it sounded like someone was sucking on a cigarette, and then the despondent man spoke again.

"He already knows he must pay the money back. Soon." He hesitated, before continuing. "It's best if the police see this as a robbery gone wrong since we have her rings."

The angry one spoke again, clearly the leader. "More should have been taken." He spoke accusingly now. "Just two rings from that house full of expensive things? *¡Eso fue un error!*" That was a mistake.

No one replied, so no way to know who he was addressing. But one thing for certain.

One of the three men being addressed by the aggressive one had killed Aurelia and taken her rings!

Tears stung my eyes, blurring my vision. I felt the salty wetness on my cheeks. With shaking hands, I put back a small piece of pottery I'd been holding, the texture rough against my fingertips.

In the process, I knocked over another piece of pottery, which, fortunately didn't fall to the ground, but the noise it made as it rattled drunkenly on the shelf caused what sounded like roof dogs above the building to bark, their yelps sending chills down my spine and catching the attention of the men.

Strange that they hadn't barked until now but maybe they'd been trained to not do so for voices since they lived above a shop? Or the dogs knew these men?

"*¿Eso qué es?*" asked one of them. The fluorescent lights overhead flickered intermittently, casting an eerie glow on everything, I now saw. It gave the space, this whole experience, an eerie feeling. Fear sent shivers down my spine, causing goosebumps on my arms.

No response came from any of them, but much shuffling took place on the gravel. Then ...

One of them hissed, his words barely audible to me, my heart hammering so. "Look, that window is open. Both of them!"

In my mind's eye, I imagined them all looking up toward the clerestory windows, shooting tension-filled glances at one another. The dogs continued to bark intermittently, just showing they were doing their jobs, their hearts not in it.

"*Ay, maldito*," muttered another voice.

"Vamos," said the aggressive one, his voice low and menacing. Let's go.

A palpable sense of danger made the hairs on the back of my neck stand up. The tension was so thick that it felt like a physical weight, pressing down on my shoulders.

I stayed frozen in the aisle, afraid to breathe, until their voices faded away. I found it hard to inhale. The smell of the pottery all around me mixed with the faint scent of cleaning solution and filled my nostrils. A part of my brain thought it odd that I hadn't noticed until now.

Only after hearing nothing but silence for a full minute did I cautiously make my way toward the front of the store, doing my best to keep my heels from clicking on the tile floor.

Had they all left? No one was coming to check in the store for the source of the noise?

The weight of tension pressed down on me, and I heard my own breathing, quick and shallow.

I stepped out of the aisle and into the open area between the start of the aisles and the shop's front door. And just then, the Follower who had confronted me outside the Gonzalez home appeared in the doorway, a dark cloud seemingly all about him—clearly not happy to see me. He was sweating profusely. The odor of fear and anger, both pungent and metallic, filled the air. Add to that the smell of sour sweat, and it nauseated me.

His stance told me he owned this shop, otherwise, how would he have felt comfortable enough to threaten someone here? He confirmed it when he looked at the cashier, ordered her to leave, to take a break, calling her by name.

This place must be a way for him to launder the proceeds from his criminal activities, for cartel business, I decided.

The young girl wasted no time, and didn't ask for an explanation. She grabbed something from under the counter, which turned out to be a Louis Vuitton monogram bag, one I couldn't help but notice was a fake, the monogram stitched crookedly. She headed out the door, and closed it behind her.

At this, my heart slammed against my ribcage, an engine in distress, pushed to its limits.

The silence in the shop was now deafening, while the light from the overhead fixtures flickered, as the man inched toward me, hands fisted at his sides.

He said nothing, but one couldn't miss the rage turning his face purple, fire shooting out of his eyes.

His footsteps, calculated and confident, slapped against the tile floor, sounding like the resonating claps of the lively hand games Manuel, Antonio, and I had played as children. I couldn't think of those two now.

I saw that The Follower thought that for sure he had me, that he could destroy me.

CHAPTER 30

I stood my ground, focusing on my breathing and the prin-
ciples of jiu-jitsu I'd learned over the past year. I knew I
had to stay calm and centered to have any chance of subdu-
ing my shorter, but much broader opponent, and most likely
stronger.

As he closed the gap between us, I observed his stance and
movements. A warm breeze came in through the clerestory
windows, and a shiver went through me despite the heat.

Now that he was closer, I could see that, actually, he favored
his left leg, which looked injured, and it left him a bit off
balance. Not as confident a stance as I had thought. He sucked
in a breath with each step he took, his injured leg struggling
to support his weight. Which gave me an opportunity.

What good fortune that, after deliberations this morning, Id
decided to wear leggings with a sleeveless tunic. It left my
arms bare, and was short enough that it wouldn't get in the
way of moving my legs. The sound of the chiffon whispered
as it brushed against my skin.

He lunged at me, his breathing heavy and labored, the scent of his sweat, and now adrenaline, increasing. I sidestepped, feeling the ground beneath my feet, solid and stable.

Using his momentum against him, with a swift, precise motion, I hooked my right foot behind his left ankle and executed a foot sweep—a move I'd done countless times in class. My muscles tensed and I felt the pressure of his weight. This move sent him stumbling forward. It surprised me that it worked the way I'd learned it would. Yet, he didn't fall to the ground.

But before he could recover, I grabbed his right arm and pulled him into a shoulder throw. His weight against mine, I felt his sweat under my hands, felt the strength of his resistance, but my own determination was stronger.

Aurelia would be avenged, and I would be married in two days! I determined this with all I had in me!

He hit the ground with a heavy thud, the wind knocked out of him. The impact vibrated through my feet, and it felt as if the ground trembled. As he lay there, gasping for breath, I felt a sense of satisfaction and relief, knowing that my training had paid off.

I didn't waste a moment. Transitioning into a side control position, I pinned his upper body with my weight. He struggled beneath me, but I remained calm and focused, despite the African drum concert going on in my chest. My poor heart! The smell of my own sweat, mixed with his, filled my nostrils, adding to the sense of urgency.

Remembering the key to jiu-jitsu, I focused on using leverage and technique rather than brute strength, which was fortunate because he was certainly stronger than me.

He grunted and managed to twist his body to try to free himself, but I was ready. I moved to a knee-on-belly position, keeping control and increasing the pressure on his chest.

His breathing became labored as he tried to buck me off, but I held on, like a *charro* holding onto one of the horses on our *hacienda*, the ones that were just being broken by professional horsemen. Still, his skin was slick with sweat, making it more difficult to maintain control. Feeling his sweat nauseated me, but I didn't let go.

With each passing moment, I could feel him weakening, his movements becoming slower and more desperate. I held on, using every ounce of my training and strength to maintain control. My own breathing grew heavier, mixing with his labored breaths, creating an odd symphony, as if we were doing a concert together.

By now, our struggle had led us near the endcap of the middle aisle of shelves.

Desperation and embarrassment on his face at the turn this was taking—he was a man, I, a woman—he threw a wild punch in my direction, which caused me to rear back, my shoulder striking the edge of a shelf with a thud.

This caused some of the pottery to tumble and crash into pieces on the floor right next to us. It unleashed a cacophony of sound and a kaleidoscope of reds, oranges, greens, and blues shards creating an island almost all around us.

Taking advantage of the distraction, he tried to punch me again. But I was ahead of him. Ignoring the pottery, though I'd end up with at least scratches if not cuts, I deflected his blow, transitioning to full mount, trapping his arm in the process. Maneuvering into an armbar, I applied pressure to his elbow joint. The heat of his skin brushed against mine, while the tension in his muscles increased as he struggled to break free.

With each movement, the sound of his labored breathing filled the room, punctuated by the occasional grunt of pain as I applied more pressure to his arm.

Despite his determination, I could feel his strength waning under the relentless pressure of the armbar. His muscles trembled, his body slick with sweat as he fought to escape.

His face twisted in pain and anger. He grunted, realizing he was caught.

He couldn't break free.

His eyes began to flutter, and his breathing became shallow and ragged, the sound of his labored gasps filling the room, along with the smell of fear ... his and mine. I could see his pulse pounding in his neck.

With each passing second, his body grew weaker, his muscles losing their tension as he drifted closer to unconsciousness.

To make sure he'd stay down, I tightened my grip a little more. I only wanted to be sure he couldn't pursue me when I escaped the shop.

His body now weak under me, his eyes not even fluttering now, his muscles gone lax, I released the hold, and jumped to my feet.

My heart raced, the sound of its beating filling my ears, while adrenaline flooded my veins. My body felt electric, muscles tense and ready for continued action.

Him being down only gave me a few precious moments, but they felt like an eternity, and were enough to give me the head start I needed to escape.

Once outside, the sun's rays bit into my skin, while the scent of dry dust and cooking spices from the corner café's kitchen, which faced this way, filled my nostrils.

Luckily, there were cars parked all along the street, their metal bodies basking in the midday sun, except for the last twenty feet or so from the intersection.

I crouched down behind the cars, my hands brushing against the warm, uneven cobblestones, and made my way to the last car nearest the intersection. My thighs screamed, a raw burn, after the fight and from moving in a crouch.

The sound of my ragged breath filled the air, a stark contrast to the lazy hum of midday on this back street. The rhythmic pounding of my heart echoed in my ears, deafening me to most other noises. The distant murmur of the traffic on Ancha San Antonio, just two blocks away, seemed as if from another world.

Then, from my spot behind the last car, the hot metal searing my thigh which was leaning on it, I saw him.

Already, he was up! He stood on the sidewalk just outside the shop, under the stark glare of the sun, bent over some, and holding on to his elbow with his opposite hand.

Just then, someone at the café must have turned on a radio or a playlist because a reggae beat filled the air, a strange contrast to what I'd just been through.

The Follower looked left and right, then gave up and disappeared into the shop—its wooden door creaking shut—no doubt to call his cronies.

I rose to my full height, my muscles protesting, quickly making my way to the corner, brushing down my clothes all the while, hoping no one from the café would spot me.

Would he dare call those other men and tell them what had happened? He'd just been bested by a *mujer* (woman), after all. The still-prevalent machismo in my country, particularly among those who did what he did for a living, might prevent him from saying anything. I hoped so. The thought was a cool balm against my adrenaline-raw nerves. It would give me time.

At the corner, I turned toward Ancha San Antonio. I didn't dare look behind me, the threat of pursuit prickling the hairs on the back of my neck.

As soon as I turned onto Ancha, I darted to the left. I crossed the street, feeling the afternoon sun hot on my back, the scent of the dry air and gasoline fumes mixing in a familiar blend.

I put my hat back on, its coarse brim rough against my fingertips, and pushed my hair inside of it. What a miracle it hadn't fallen out of my tote, which I'd been able to grab while making my escape! Its leather straps dug into my shoulder, a comforting weight.

I walked into Mercado Sano, a location bustling with multiple health shops, and with an upstairs. The scent of fresh produce, coffee, and essential oils burning diffusers washed over me. I could get lost in here, in the murmur of voices and clatter of shopping being done, and then come out its side door, and head back toward my house or my shop. Well, my house, of course.

I couldn't face Esme and Sofia, both working today, both thinking me deep in wedding preparations. Not walking around town disheveled after putting my jiu-jitsu moves to the test! My muscles ached, still thrumming with the adrenaline of the fight.

The whole time, my heart pounded, a drum against my rib cage, a refrain matching it in my head.

They killed Aurelia.

They killed Aurelia.

My breath hitched with each repetition—the taste of fear metallic on my tongue.

I hurried upstairs, slipped into a restroom, and splashed water on my face, the shock of it momentarily grounding me. My hands shook, the tremors visible in the stark white light. Looking at myself in the small mirror above the sink, I wished for Manuel. No. I could not tell him any of this! He'd be so angry. His image in my mind gave me a sharp pang, an almost physical sensation.

But, also, how could I *not* tell him? My indecision churned inside me like a storm.

No matter what, I had enough solid information to give to Antonio. Enough that he could bring them all in and question them, and figure out who, among them, the killer was.

In the end, any of the three from today could have been Balaclava Man. The thought sent another chill down my spine. Three possible men who might want to kill me for witnessing that exit from Ramon and Aurelia's house.

CHAPTER 31

After I made it home there was almost no time to shower before Luna arrived, both of us eager to keep working on the journal, our final chance to do so before the whirlwind of my wedding the day after tomorrow.

When her silhouette filled my doorway, I couldn't help but envelop her in a warm hug, the familiar scent of her signature musky perfume a comforting balm after the day's traumas.

We climbed the stairs to my main floor, heading straight to the kitchen island, where we poured ourselves each a glass of rich, ruby-red wine. The first sip seeped down into my bone marrow loosening the knots in my shoulders.

"So, *chica*, what you been up to, huh?" Luna twirled her wine glass by the stem, looking at me with curiosity.

I gave her a where-to-start-look.

"What if we get started while I tell you everything I know so far?" I suggested, reaching for my glass.

"Oh, lots to say?" Excitement lit up her eyes as she leaned forward, her hands clasping together in anticipation.

"Yes, Luna. *Lots* to say." I tried to mask my anxiety, recalling the fight.

We moved to the dining room table where the journal pages and their fragments waited. They fluttered a bit as we continued to piece them together. We now had six pages, each in a different stage of completion. We agreed to only read them once they were all reconstructed.

To the soothing strains of a Chopin melody coming from my iPhone speakers—I had needed something to calm me after the day—I told Luna everything I now knew about The Followers, Pablo's gambling, the conversation I'd overheard this afternoon, the memory of that menacing tone still lingering in my ears, how one of The Followers had found me in the shop—and how we'd fought.

When I got to that part, Luna shot up with the force of a Space X rocket leaving Earth for Mars, the sound of her chair scraping against the wood floor adding an exclamation point to her action.

"OH MY GOODNESS, *chica*, you followed him? You *fought* with him? *¿En qué estabas pensando?*" What were you thinking.

I had no answer to that, uncertainty now fluttering around my heart region. I tugged at the long sleeve of my t-shirt, adjusting it to be sure Luna wouldn't see a bruise on my forearm, a souvenir from my skirmish with that man. Thank goodness my face had been spared.

"You should have called!" She raised her arms in a gesture of unmistakable frustration.

"Call? What, between the first and second kicks? There was no time. Plus, at first I didn't even know I was going to follow him. And I definitely didn't know we'd be fighting." I looked at the table instead of at my angry friend.

She sat back down. "*Chica*, one of these days, these risks you take are going to catch up with you ..." She picked up a fragment and looked for a place where it might fit.

"I'm okay, Luna. I didn't *plan* it. And look how much I found out!"

She shook her head, a hesitant look on her face as if she was about to say something, but just then, firecrackers went off outside somewhere, puncturing the tension between us, and just like that, it evaporated, landing us in a companionable enough silence.

We had mutely agreed to disagree, and continued the work of putting the pieces together, the only sound the faint rustle of the paper, and more firecrackers in the distance.

In the semi-quiet, my mind went over everything I had to tell Antonio.

At least, I had an idea on how to do that now without putting myself immediately in the line of fire of what was sure to be an epic anger episode, even for him.

I looked at my phone to see the time. Gilberto, a young man who sometimes ran errands for me was coming in an hour to get the pages and drop them off at the police station.

He couldn't come any later and there was no time to finish this, and also write down everything I discovered about Aurelia's murder before Gilberto got here.

No way could I call Antonio to tell him what I knew. I cringed at the thought of his reaction and about how he'd tell Manuel.

"So, out of the three, who do you think did it?" Luna asked, her voice soft and inquisitive, Dap back in her lap and purring.

"It's hard to tell ..." I held a small piece of paper aloft, gazing off toward the kitchen, thinking. "Balaclava Man could have been any of them, that's the thing."

"It's funny how you give names like that to them. Balaclava Man, The Followers. You're like those journalists who make up names for celebrity couples. You know, TomKat, Bennifer, and like that." Her laughter rang warm and bright.

"Well, I don't know their names, and I have to call them something."

We giggled, the familiar sound of our shared laughter bringing me a sense of comfort. Luna always brought out my playful side, no matter what else was going on.

Still, my mind raced back to who the culprit might be. "Can you imagine the mess in Pablo and Leonora's marriage once she knows that his gambling caused all this?" The very thought sent a shiver down my spine.

"*Ay*, that will be bad, I agree. Do you think Pablo would confess to her about it now? Before the police tell her? So she gives him the money? I mean ..." She trailed off, looking back at me, her eyes skeptical.

"Well, I doubt Pablo wants to confess to Leonora, but what choice does he have?" I reached for my wine glass and took a cautious sip, pondering the situation. "I think that after what I heard this afternoon, he's going to have to. Whoever his contact among those men is, he's bound to know real soon that he'll be killed unless he pays. So, with his life on the line, she'd certainly give him the money. Wouldn't you?" I added, convinced.

"But, wait. Once she finds out that the men he owed money to killed her mother, wouldn't she be more likely to divorce him than to pay his debt? That's what I'd do!" She wanted me to agree, I could see it in her eyes. "I mean, we women at least have the right to keep our inheritances to ourselves even if we're married, correct?" She leaned in, plainly eager for my insight.

"Correct. But, Luna, even if she didn't give him the money, do you think the cartel would let it go so easy? And even if they got a divorce, I doubt she'd want her child's father to be murdered by brutes. And let's not forget, the cartel would kill her, probably kill her child in front of her first, unless she paid ..."

I gazed at her to see if this connected. "But I don't think it matters. None of that will happen because now they'll all get arrested."

I felt a moment of pride that I had something to do with that, and finished aligning another piece of the journal and taped it down.

"Oh ... true ..." She nodded in contemplation.

"I'll get everything I know to the *real* detective. He's not *estúpido*, my cousin." I glanced at her, a wry smile on my face. "He'll figure out the rest."

She smiled, as if proud of him for that. Luna liked Antonio. Her gaze drifted off, a dreamy look crossing her face. I was beginning to think that she liked him a lot, actually ...

Brushing that aside for now, I grinned, feeling a blush creep up my face. "After all, I have a rehearsal dinner to attend tomorrow night, and a wedding the day after that. Mine! *Ay*!"

Excited, she raised her wine glass towards mine. "Yes!" she exclaimed. Our glasses clinked, the sound echoing through the room.

I asked if she wanted a refill. She shook her head solemnly, placing her glass back on the table with care.

"Oh, no, *gracias*. My best friend's wedding is the day after tomorrow, and there's a rehearsal dinner tomorrow night and we're going to the spa in the afternoon. I want to be clear-headed." She smirked at me.

I burst out laughing and she followed suit, our chuckles filling the room. I leaned back, stretching my arms above my head before resuming our task. Gilberto would be here soon, so we needed to focus.

After another minute or so, Luna stopped what she was doing and looked at me, a quizzical look on her face. She tilted her head to the side, a small smile playing on her lips as she tapped a finger on the table.

"What?" I asked, looking up, curious about her sudden silence.

"No sé, chica. Things always seem to go your way when it comes time to solve mysteries." Her voice was playful, a hint of admiration in her tone.

It made me feel shy. A sudden breeze from the open living room window caused the pages to move around, and I placed my hand over them.

"I don't know ... can I go over it all again, just to be sure I have it right?" I asked, my eyes scanning the fragmented pages. We were nearly there.

"Claro." Of course. She leaned back in her chair, crossing her arms, preparing to listen.

"Here we have Pablo getting into debt with a cartel about six months ago because of his gambling. Then, he gets arrested in a raid of an underground gambling place."

Luna nodded her head, her eyes flickering to her phone, mindful of the time.

"Then, he begins to owe too much money to them to ever pay it back because they keep adding to the interest. And, of course, the cartel gets impatient."

I shifted in my chair. Then, something dawned on me. Why were they being so patient with Pablo, I wondered. That missing piece that kept escaping me, the feeling of it, came back.

That's when it hit me like a pedestrian knocking into me on our busy streets, like the Red Sea had parted and I could now see to the other side of this whole mess.

I jerked back, and gasped, slapping a hand on my thigh.

Luna stared at me, confused. "What? What happened?"

Putting up a finger to indicate she should wait a moment, I closed my eyes, took a deep breath to calm myself, but also to try and get the memory back. Had I really seen that?

When I'd left the Gonzalez home the last time, the children playing in clear view of the hall table, me gazing at it, wishing I could leave the FedEx envelope on it, I'd glanced at the family photos there.

One had stuck with me, except it had somehow remained hidden in the way back of my mind.

A photo of Pablo, his arm slung around another man's shoulders.

And then, like numbered balls falling into the slots of a bingo cage, things fell into place.

"Carli, you freaking me out, *chica*. What is it?" Luna asked, her voice tense.

I opened my eyes and looked at her.

"Oh, Luna ..." I trailed off.

Her face said it all. She was out of patience with me.

"What if ..." I was thinking out loud. "What if Pablo had a twin? An *identical* twin?" I glanced at my now speechless friend.

"It would explain so much." I checked to see if she saw the possibility.

"I saw a photo of him at the house," I said, nodding my head in the direction of my neighbors' house, "and in it, Pablo has his arm around the shoulders of a man who looks ... just like him!"

"*¡Dios mío!*" Whispered Luna. My goodness.

I sucked in a breath. Luna seemed to be frozen in place in her chair. My eyes drifted toward my kitchen window, toward the Gonzalez home with its beautiful garden.

How could I find out if Pablo had a twin without causing suspicion?

"That would mean, what?" Asked Luna, clearly thinking out loud. "That means there's four suspects instead of three, *si*?"

I nodded. Yes, four suspects. "Maybe he's that Santiago, the one mentioned in that FedEx letter." I nodded in the direction of my closet where I'd stashed it. "It makes sense. The letter threatened his family, and if Santiago was his brother, he'd be in danger too. And it said that they know where he lives." I exhaled forcefully through my mouth. "Don't you see? It's why Pablo seemed so different to me when I saw him in El Jardin with The Followers. *That's* who I saw there, his twin. *Not* Pablo."

I thought for a moment and, nodding in the direction of the Gonzalez house, I added, "I'm not taking that letter back there. I'll give it to Antonio instead."

We gazed at one another, both our minds working overtime, putting together this new puzzle. "I'll bet they work together! The brother and those men. It would explain the argument and everything they said today, too."

"Sure, I can see that ..." Her voice was soft, distant, thinking all this out.

"I think the twin's role in all this is leaning on Pablo to pay back the money." It all fell into place in my head. I couldn't sit, so I got up and paced around the dining room table, while Luna stared at me, mouth partially open. I stopped right in front of her.

"So, Pablo goes into debt, they keep raising the interest, Pablo can't pay, the *jefe* starts to lean on The Followers because it must be their job to collect, and they bring in his brother who happens to work with them. Then ..." I swallowed. "Then, one of them kills Aurelia for money."

I stopped and whirled toward her. "So Leonora could give Pablo money for his debt ..." I trailed off.

Luna nodded, still wordless. The ice maker on the refrigerator chose this moment to clatter ice into the container and we both jumped. But I was onto something and went on.

"I'll bet he's a lower ranked member of their organization. The twin, I mean. The Followers, too." I sat back down.

Luna finally found her voice. "Why lower-ranked?" She leaned forward, elbows resting on the table.

"Because they wouldn't be doing what they're doing, like killing Aurelia, if they were at least *tenientes*." Lieutenants. I shrugged, glancing down at the journal, but not seeing it.

"So, I think that they're either *halcónes*, enforcers, or *sicarios*, hitmen." My eyes met hers, seeking confirmation of my theory.

"It doesn't matter which. The point is that they're involved in Aurelia's murder, and most likely killed her. One of them did, or Pablo." My mind went to memories of Aurelia, coming into my shop, waving at me when we happened to cross one another on the street, or at the markets, and I felt my eyes sting. Perhaps it was best that Ramon had died first—he might not have survived knowing that this had happened to his beloved wife.

We said nothing for a few minutes. Then, we happened to look down and realized that we'd put together all the pages of the journal.

Our eyes locked. Letting out a whoop, we stood and went into the living room, throwing ourselves into the depths of my couch, shoulders touching, holding the pages between us so we could read them at the same time.

CHAPTER 32

The next morning—the day before my wedding—I bolted straight up in bed as soon as I woke up. The sheets rustled beneath me, the faint scent of lavender from my laundry detergent scenting the air, making me want to burrow back into the cocoon of my bed.

The commotion made Dap cranky, and he let me know with a throaty, furious meow. His soft, warm presence slid away from my side.

The whole episode from yesterday afternoon, and what the journal pages had revealed came back to me in a rush, with the force of a sudden gust of wind blowing in from seemingly nowhere, the kind that can knock you to the ground.

I'd solved the mystery of the skeleton!

And Aurelia's murder! Well, almost. I still didn't know which of the possible culprits had done it. Or why. Not for certain.

Meanwhile, this is what the journal had revealed to us.

... Also, there is my family's investment. If they find out how Alberto's father got the money to invest, everyone involved will be angry, fearful. None of them want to be involved in cartel business.

The two buildings we're buying to construct those studio apartments for expats and those so-called digital nomads cost so much to buy and renovate. We are all pulling our money together, and this is no time to have the thing fall apart on us, because what if the police discover that Alberto's father is investing with us? Using cartel funds that his son gave him?

Alberto told me last night how he gave his father money for his portion of that investment. Carlos, Alberto's father, one of my favorite uncles, hadn't said. I assumed he'd had the money in savings. Why would he ask his son, a cartel man, for money to invest in our family project?

This had, of course, startled me. So much so, that one shot of tequila had led to another. What was to have been one or two shots with my cousin for old time's sake, turned out to be half the bottle!

He called saying he was just thirty minutes away from San Miguel, on his way back to Mexico City from Guanajuato, and was thinking of stopping by. With my wife and daughter out of town for a few days, and no work the next day, I'd thought why not? I'll have a shot of tequila with my cousin who came to visit impromptu. He too, must miss our friendship as I sometimes did.

Just a moment of weakness, me reminiscing about the good times Alberto and I had had before he got all involved in that cartel business. What a mistake.

At least, Alberto happened to tell me that he'd told no one he was coming to San Miguel, that he'd decided on the spur of the moment. I didn't mind that as I'd rather the cartel didn't know one of their members was visiting me.

But that, him telling me about giving my uncle money ... that I minded. Very much. Would I have told the others? What would they have thought? Too late to think of that now. But without my uncle's share of the investment, the project couldn't move forward. We were all counting on it, my other uncle and aunt having put their retirement savings into it as a way to increase those savings, something to live on in their old age.

Alberto looked rougher than I remembered. Of course, I haven't seen him in at least five years. I'd distanced myself from him, and perhaps he knew why because he hadn't pushed me when I'd kept claiming to be too busy to see him all those times he called soon after I found out how he made his money.

So, we continued to drink tequila, both of us unsteady after several shots, each bringing up boyhood pranks we'd engaged in, such as the time we took his father's car keys as teenagers. Neither of us with a driver's license yet, but we were bold, and thought the world would always be kind to us.

At one point, loud music reached us from next door where a party seemed to be starting. We could hear more and more voices over the ten-foot wall, and now the music.

Everything from this moment on happened very fast. So fast, I couldn't get my head around it.

Alberto turned his head toward the noise. At the same time, he half-rose from his seat, reaching for the bottle of tequila. As he did, his foot caught on a leg of his chair. This whole time he was singing along to the pop song coming from next door.

Then, his voice silenced ... forever, it turned out, his skull sounding like a pumpkin cracking open as it hit the concrete of the patio.

I couldn't move, instead staring at the blood flowing from Alberto's head. If I'd moved fast, could I have saved him? His glazed eyes told me no. So drunk I was, so drunk. I know it because the first thing I thought of was whether if I moved fast, I could hose down the patio and keep the blood from staining the concrete.

I feel ashamed now. My cousin was dead and I thought of my patio. I am never again drinking tequila.

Even worse is that I had a moment when somehow I knew that Alberto was about to get hurt. A few seconds when I might have been able to do something, to reach out and steady him. Sadness fills me now thinking about that. Sure, the tequila slowed me down, but this was my cousin, once my best friend.

It frightened me, having him dead there on the ground right in front of me, his dead eyes on mine.

I leaned down and shut his eyelids, nearly falling on top of him in the process.

Next door, the music continued as if a man hadn't just died. The strangeness of the situation, my dead cousin at my feet, I sobered up enough to move around, but not quite as much as might have been good for me.

However, what else could I have done? No way could I have called the police. What if it came out about Alberto giving money to his father for our project? They would at a minimum want that money. Then, we'd all lose out. The police might even take all our money, somehow deciding that it linked to Alberto. It wasn't unknown for police to help themselves to the money of others, under a flimsy excuse or another.

I remembered that Alberto had told me he'd come on the spur of the moment, that no one knew. And as a single man, no one waited for him at home.

Thinking about all that, and under the influence of the tequila I am never drinking again, I buried my cousin in my garden, in the back of it by the fence, where it was gravel on the ground. This way, it was easier to hide the hole once I put the gravel back after moving it to dig the grave.

It took me a long time to dig the hole, put him in it, and cover it up. After that, I said the usual funeral prayers, a Padre Nuestro and Ave Maria pleading that my cousin's soul be forgiven and not held in purgatory or sent to hell, that he be pardoned by God despite his mistakes.

Even now, twenty-four hours later, I still feel dirty from him, from touching a dead body, despite the three showers I've taken since then.

My poor cousin. I threw out all of the tequila in the house. Agatha won't ask; she never goes near it.

Of course, when I woke this morning and all this came back to me, I wished I'd called the police, but it was too late.

How would I explain the fact that I'd buried him in my garden? Why would they not think that I pushed him, that it was my fault he was dead?

And then, the investment money. No, I could not unearth Alberto and call the police now. I would have to carry this guilt for the rest of my life.

If the police are told now, and if I am charged with murder and taken to jail—a certainty when the cops see the dirt on Alberto and the hole in the garden—then the cartel will think I killed Alberto, and they'll come kill me, and Agatha and our daughter, surely.

So, no. I could not notify the police about Alberto's death.

Alberto wasn't much loved in my family. Other than his parents, not too many would miss him. I would grieve him, but not for long. Our initial bond was gone. It could even be said that him disappearing could be expected. He'd gone bad and so everyone in the family had turned their backs on him.

They would think the cartel had done something, or that he'd run away to escape them. Plus, Alberto was known, to go off on the spur of the moment and not get in touch, sometimes for weeks at a time. No one wanted to know what he did during these expeditions of his.

It will be several weeks before rumors begin about where he might be. In time, they will all find it easier to believe that perhaps Alberto left Mexico, maybe went and got himself lost in Belize or Brazil to escape the cartel. They'll think he might have done something wrong. Even I knew that in those organizations you did what the jefe told you. Otherwise ...

I must resign myself to the fact that Alberto is buried in my backyard. And that I can't call the police. I must act normal when my wife and child come home tomorrow. It will be my cross to bear.

A terribly sad story, but at least Sofia's favorite uncle had not killed a man. He'd only buried one, which he'd have to account for, of course, but it wasn't the same as killing him.

After we were done reading, we made copies on my home printer, and placed the originals in a plain brown envelope, the kind used for business documents. Inside, we placed the reconstructed pages, and a note that these were journal pages taken from Eduardo Caldero's home that appeared to belong to him. So that Antonio wouldn't recognize my handwriting or Luna's, we printed the note.

We then printed a sheet of crisp, white paper with Antonio's name in big letters on the front, and his title, *Sargento de Investigación* on it. And under that, *URGENTE*.

Of course, our fingerprints were all over the journal and the envelope, but the chances of Antonio asking to fingerprint Luna and me were slim enough that we were okay taking that chance.

Gilberto had arrived just as we were finishing. He'd delivered the envelope to a nearby police station, then texted to let me know it was done.

So this morning, I thought Antonio could wrap up the whole case about the skeleton before tomorrow.

And if he got the information I had on the Aurelia case early enough today, maybe even solve her murder? I mean he just had to interrogate a few men, and he had help, he didn't have to do it all himself.

I brushed aside the fact that the men in question were not likely to fall apart and confess without a lot of strong arming. And that before they could be interrogated, they had to be found ...

In any case, I felt grateful that my cousin would be too busy to worry just yet about how he was getting all this information.

He'd suspect me, but between Eduardo and the skeleton, Aurelia's murder, Ramon's death, the double killings in La Lejona, and my wedding tomorrow which he had to attend, no choice in that if he wanted to remain a part of our family, plus him being best man, learning where the envelope had come from would be low on his list.

He'd assign the task to a detective or a police officer and when they didn't find our fingerprints in their database, he'd most likely let it go. For now.

I stretched, then curled up again hugging a pillow to my chest, enjoying the feel of its soft fabric against my skin.

Still, much to do today. This afternoon was Ana's spa for much pampering for all the women in my wedding party. Couldn't wait!

It would be *divine*. I loved being spoiled like that, and Ana's spa provided the best treatments, the whole place always wrapped in the delicate scents of lavender and eucalyptus, the ultimate relaxing experience.

And at four o'clock was the rehearsal, yes, early, but we wanted everyone to be able to rest before the next day.

By three o'clock in the afternoon tomorrow, I would be Manuel's Mrs, and he, my Mr.—this made me chuckle.

It dawned on me just then that as of tomorrow, I'd be sleeping with Manuel most nights, and waking up next to him, his deep, soothing voice being the first thing I'd hear every day.

I felt the blush start at my toes and work its way up to my hairline. I buried my face in the pillow and screamed in happiness and embarrassment, the muffled sound vibrating against my cheeks.

But, I still had that one thing left to do before I focused only on my big day. It made my heart race in anticipation.

CHAPTER 33

I could no longer just lie around in the soft sheets of my bed. Too much to do. I got up and headed to the kitchen.

Gazing at the Gonzalez garden while the water got to the perfect temperature, I felt a deep sadness for the Gonzalez children. Their lives had already been shaken considerably. And they were about to be shaken even more when they discovered why their mother had been killed. And who had killed her.

Because time was short, I went to my desk and booted up my laptop, thinking of my task while the laptop's fans hummed as they got going.

Dap, confused, stood near me, letting out a couple of plaintive meows.

"So sorry, Dapperoo. There's no time to go to the roof this morning. Mamá has things to do. We're solving a murder, you know! And then ..." I stopped here, turned in my chair which creaked a little beneath me, and looked down into his brilliant green eyes.

"Tomorrow, I will be married. Tía Luna will come to take care of you while me and your new daddy go on a short honeymoon, okay? You know him, it's Manuel, you like him! He gives you too many treats. Yes, that *vato*." I scratched behind his ear as I told him all this.

He looked as if he were considering my words, as if he wondered whether he should allow it. Then, he walked away from me slowly, someone who mattered not at all to him, tail way up in the air, brushing against my legs before leaving. I shook my head and returned to my most important task.

I wrote down the conversation I had overheard yesterday, recalling every word as best as I could, the keys on my laptop clicking as I typed. Where my memory faltered, I paraphrased, ensuring that every detail, as I remembered it, was captured on the page.

What I'd discovered about Pablo and the money he owed. About his twin, The Followers, and the Aggressive One. There, a name for him, too. I described The Followers, wrote that Pablo's brother looked just like him, and that I had no idea what the aggressive man looked like.

I mentioned that there were online articles about Pablo having been arrested six months ago for gambling illegally.

And then, I put down what I thought had happened, why I thought Aurelia had been killed.

It was so that Leonora could get her inheritance and give money to Pablo to pay his debts back.

Next, I looked up Jorge's email address which he included in all his bylines. After creating a new email address for myself under a different name, I sent Jorge everything I'd written, my hands shaking.

He would likely add a link to the article he'd written about people who owed money to *cartels* and how they dealt with the debts. Though Antonio must know that already.

This information solved the case for Antonio. All he had to do was bring in Pablo's brother, and The Followers if he could find them hanging around as they had been the past week, their footsteps haunting the streets of my favorite city, my home, and that of all my favorite people. The nerve of them!

Antonio would, in time, figure out it was me who had given the information to Jorge, and then also realize that I'd sent the journal pages to him, but I'd deal with that later, the thought of it causing tension to build in my chest. Well, it wouldn't be the first time Antonio and I confronted one another over the solving of mysteries.

But it would be the last. Had to be. I was about to be Manuel's wife after all, and that meant no more sleuthing.

Jorge would know right away I'd sent the email based on our meeting and our talk about his article. But, because I sent the message anonymously, he'd treat it the same way he treated his other sources by protecting my identity.

With a flourish, and holding my breath, I clicked the blue arrow to send the message.

The message that solved it all.

I couldn't help the grin that plastered itself on my face, the warmth of excitement spreading across my cheeks.

Now, it was time to let it all go and get myself married! The anticipation filled me with love, my heart blooming like a big red rose.

CHAPTER 34

TWO WEEKS LATER

Manuel and I dashed around my kitchen, or, I should say, *our* kitchen, deciding on everything we wanted taken up to the roof, the scent of spices and garlic filling the air. He had prepared light appetizers and his signature chicken mole for our guests.

I had set the dining table with yellow, red, and orange napkins, and plates in the same colors, their glazed surfaces waiting to be filled with the delicious foods made by my husband. I loved saying that, *my husband*.

In the center, a large bouquet of orange marigolds and yellow dahlias from the hacienda held court.

Antonio would be here tonight, and I prepared myself for an earful, because, of course, he'd now figured out where the information to make his arrests had come from. At least, Manuel was here to run interference if need be.

I couldn't wait to see Antonio who hadn't taken my calls and only replied to my texts in monosyllables since the wedding. Tonight, he'd be telling us all what had happened after he got the journal and the information about who might have murdered Aurelia. Jorge had been quick to get it to him.

We still didn't know for sure who had killed her. The men had been arrested, but the killer not yet disclosed. Antonio knew who, as of this morning, and the right man had been charged with murder. This would be in tomorrow's newspaper. But we'd find out tonight.

We also didn't know whether Eduardo had been arrested, whether he was in prison, or under house arrest.

As soon as I went back to work after the wedding, Sofia had called to say that she needed to take time off urgently because of "an important family matter." She didn't disclose that it was about Eduardo and the skeleton. The family had closed ranks and were speaking to no one about the matter. Considering this was Sofia not talking, it said a lot about how seriously they were taking this. I'd had to hire a friend of Esme's to replace her, at least temporarily. I hoped she would come back once Eduardo's fate was clear.

On the day before my wedding, after I'd emailed Jorge, things had quickly spiraled.

The first I heard was from *mamá* who texted to tell me that Antonio reached out to tell her he might be late to the rehearsal. And that he might not be able to stay for dinner after, or he'd stay but would leave early, and did I know something about that.

My heart caused quite a commotion in my rib cage as I replied.

> No, Mamá.

I immediately sent another text, this one to Luna.

> It's in motion, chica!

She'd responded right away that she thought it was great.

> ¡Genial!

That afternoon, before dinner, we'd followed our plan and visited the spa. The pampering left us all feeling blissfully relaxed, each of us sporting new manicures and pedicures in soft blush polish. Even Luna-of-the-usually-loud-polish agreed to that, can you believe it?

Antonio arrived at the rehearsal just as we were all standing around the altar, some of the wedding flowers already delivered and scenting the air.

He apologized in earnest for his tardiness, eyes heavy with speculation when they landed on me. I did my best to keep a flush from rising to my cheeks.

After the meal, he downed his espresso in one gulp, refused dessert and said he had to go, that he was going back to work because he had people to "interview."

Antonio's gaze landed on me as he said it, the suspicion in his eyes unmistakable.

My mother berated him for leaving, her voice soft and concerned. He never took his eyes off me. What? Would he have preferred that I'd sent him the information *after* the wedding? All the suspects would have been long gone by then. Sheesh.

The next day, well, what can one say? I remember my wedding day in snapshots more than anything. You know, like those videos that flicker from image to image and all you're left with at the end is the overall feelings you felt while they played?

Thanks to our *mamás'* careful planning, it all went without a glitch. The train of my dress caught a bit on the stone staircase while I walked up down the steps for photos after leaving the church, but no damage done. My bridesmaids pulled it up, shook it out a bit, the silk crunching between their fingers, and I continued on down.

My heart full of joy, batting my eyes to keep from crying, I clung to both my father and mother's arms, cherishing our Mexican tradition of both parents walking their child down the aisle.

The aroma of incense and beeswax candles filled the air as we waited at the back of the church for my bridesmaids to make it to the front, and for the music that would accompany my walk down the aisle to my beloved to begin. Our guests all stood to watch me.

I hadn't seen the inside since the rehearsal, and now was awed by how it had been transformed. The end of each pew held a large bouquet of gardenias, roses, dahlias, and baby's breath, their sweet fragrance wafting through the space.

On the floor, a floral ribbon made of the same flowers started at the last pew in the back and gracefully extended all the way to the first pew in front on both sides of the center aisle.

To the sound of *Stand By Me* played on the violin by my cousin Carmen, this being the first song Manuel and I had ever danced to as teens, I took my first step down this fairy-tale aisle, and toward my future.

That future, in the form of Manuel, waited for me at the altar, his eyes glistening, while I batted mine to avoid a mascara incident despite Ana having assured me it was waterproof.

Three of my much younger cousins walked down the aisle ahead of us, their tiny footsteps like whispers on the church floor, dropping white and pink petals, creating a magical look-ing pathway for me to glide on.

When we reached my most handsome fiancé, both my mother and father hugged him, then hugged me, and with tears in their eyes, went to take their seat.

Manuel stood with the bearing of a king of old, staring at me with wide, startled, and loving eyes. Passion burned from them, too. The intensity of his gaze could no doubt scorch if not controlled. The heat of it made my knees buckle.

Trembling with emotion, I stood next to him, finding it diffi-cult to believe my incredible fortune. Only the warmth of his hand in mine made everything real.

Before I knew it, I'd said yes, Manuel had said yes, and we'd both cried a little while our families and friends stood and applauded, their cheers echoing all around.

Afterward, our *callejoneada* went superbly, the sounds of laughter and joy reverberating through the cobblestone streets. The only hiccup was the donkey carrying the small kegs of tequila getting stubborn at one point and refusing to move forward. This brought lots of laughs from our group of about fifty, our chuckles mingling with the ongoing mariachi music. After much braying and a few gentle nudges, the donkey decided to keep walking after all.

My father and Manuel's had filled those kegs with the best *añejo* tequila from our family *tequileria*. The rich, amber liquid glided into the *caballitos—tequila* glasses—filling the nostrils of all who drank it with its warm, inviting scent. As our guests sipped the tequila, their smiles grew wider, and the lively energy of the group caught the attention of many passersby who took the time to stop and applaud us.

Later, with everyone having arrived at the hacienda, our celebration was in full swing, Manuel and I pulled everywhere at once by relatives and friends who wanted to congratulate us, even the ones who'd already done so, either at the church or during our *callejoneada*.

Despite all that, I took a moment to look around me.

The setting and ambiance couldn't have been more perfect. In this area of our property, between my parents' and Manuel's parents' house, numerous citrus trees thrived, primarily producing *limón*, their delightful aroma detectible on the soft breeze.

With our houses nestled far from the busy highway, I knew that if my wedding reception weren't happening right now, we'd hear the occasional soft bleating of our goats, or roosters crowing, or the rhythmic hum of tractors being used to diligently tend to duties across the vast expanse of the property. And of course, the *charros*—the men who worked with our horses and did ranch work—calling out to one another in the distance. Ranch sounds. Sounds I'd grown up hearing every day, sounds that meant peace, that meant home, to me.

But instead of that, we heard the loud joyous celebration. There was the traditional music played by a twelve-member

mariachi band working its way around the large area dedicat-
ed to the reception. Later, a local band had played the popular
music of today and from many years ago to keep everyone
happy.

And the children! So many children, the younger ones chasing
one another, their laughter filling the air, no matter how many
times their parents tried to get them to settle down.

Just before midnight, Manuel and I had finally left for our
mini honeymoon at the vineyard. But our exit did not go
unnoticed.

The mariachi band lined up along the driveway, and played
and sang perhaps a little louder than they had earlier. After
all, they'd been drinking excellent tequila.

From somewhere deeper on the property, firecrackers and
small fireworks were set off, lending excitement to the joyous
chaos of it all.

All the members of our families circled around us, dozens of
people who all wanted to say goodbye and to wish us luck,
again.

I would never forget the beauty of this night, not ever.

An hour later, Manuel and I had fallen into our bed at the
winery after pushing aside the rose petals that covered it. We
ignored the bottle of champagne waiting in the ice bucket
with two crystal flutes next to it on a large silver tray.

So exhausted were we that we fell into the cloud-like bed fully
clothed—I'd changed into a loose Zadig&Voltaire mastic color
Riciny Courtney Dress an hour before we left our reception
because I'd been so full of all the food I'd eaten. I could
sleep in this dress, and it's exactly what I did, too tired to be

embarrassed or shy about falling into bed with Manuel. My husband.

He had pulled me into his arm and kissed me on the lips, the head, the cheeks, then pulled me closer. We had both fallen into a deep sleep, our limbs intertwined like the branches of the Montezuma cypress trees that grew on our *hacienda*.

Our true wedding night had had to wait ...

CHAPTER 35

N ow, standing in our kitchen and hearing the doorbell ring, I braced myself for Antonio.

But Luna arrived first. She gave Manuel a big hug, enveloping him in her arms. As if her huge aura and the scent of her perfume weren't enough, just one look at what she'd chosen to wear for a quiet dinner with friends on my roof deck, and no one could deny we were in the presence of a woman with Presence, yes, with a capital P.

She had on a Vivienne Westwood off-the-shoulder tartan wool corset top with matching wide bottom pants. Which she wore with orange So Me Red Sole tonal spike leather sandals by Louboutin. She carried a matching tote bag with a red cashmere throw peeking out of it.

The warm, melodic tone of her voice brushed against my ears.

She greeted Manuel first. "So, *guapo*, you taking care of my girl?" Good-looking.

Manuel and I laughed out loud at this, the sound of our mirth echoing in the kitchen, blending with the moving around of pans on the stove by Maria, a sous-chef from Manuel's restaurant, "stolen" from there for the evening, along with Umberto, a server.

Luna grinned, lifting her eyebrows and her chin at him, her silent query lingering in the warm kitchen air, signaling she expected an answer.

"He is, Luna, he is," I said before Manuel could answer her—the softness and gratitude in my own voice surprising even me, as it floated through the kitchen like a gentle breeze.

Manuel, stepping back from the hug, but still hanging on to her arms like a lifeline, looked her right in the eye while he answered her, his voice deep and steadfast, the promise in it strong and unbreakable as iron.

"She's the most precious thing to me, nothing bad will ever happen to her until I take my last breath."

They stared at one another for a moment, and I watched, fascinated, my eyes tearing.

"Bueno," she said, her voice ringing with acceptance, and then added "So, let's get this party started, huh?" The anticipation in her voice shone through, amplifying the buzz in the kitchen.

"Yes!" Manuel and I exclaimed at the same time, both of us energized even more by her enthusiasm.

We filed upstairs then, the collective sound of our shoes creating a rhythm on the concrete stairs, but halfway to the roof, Manuel turned around to go back down to the front door because the doorbell had just gone off again, its tinny jingle slicing through the house.

Minutes after Luna and I stepped onto the deck, we heard voices and the sound of two sets of footsteps, a robust duet that ricocheted off the high concrete walls of the stairwell. Sure enough, Antonio soon appeared in the doorframe, Manuel right behind him.

"Antonio! So happy to see you." I exclaimed, going for an all-is-good-between-us vibe. I went to him and did the cheek-kiss thing, inhaling a faint hint of aftershave lingering on his skin, a sharp and clean scent.

"Carli, *hola*," he responded, though not as enthusiastically as he might have before I "interfered with his investigations," as he liked to call what I did.

Not always grateful, that one, I mused, a touch of amusement flickering within me. By the end of the night, I would have won him back, I felt certain of it.

"All we need now is Amy and Douglas and we can start feasting and Antonio, you can tell us all what happened," I quipped, my words fluttering playfully in the cooling air.

From under the weight of heavy lids, Antonio gazed at me, the corners of his mouth quivering. It looked to me like a sliver of sunlight peeking through a dark cloud. A wave of relief washed over me.

"What if I don't tell you anything?" He teased, his voice carrying the soft burr of jest, his eyes glinting.

"What? You wouldn't dare!" Luna chimed in; her tone threaded in playful challenge.

Antonio looked at her, grinning wide. "Well, if you dare me, I'll have to accept that." He crossed his arms, and kept his eyes on her, tongue in cheek.

"No, no! I take it back. You WOULD dare, I know it. Ignore what I said. *Por favor*!" Luna was begging, and it made us all laugh.

The doorbell pierced through our airy chatter, and soon, Amy and Douglas joined us, everyone greeting them with hugs and cheek kisses.

Firecrackers went off a street or two over, as if in celebration of our get-together and the end of the mayhem that had plagued us.

Everyone sat in great timing, as Maria and Umberto arrived on the roof with platters that held the promising aroma of various appetizers.

Manuel uncorked bottles of special reserve red wine, and its rich dark berry scent combined with the smell of the food, all promised a relaxed evening of fine dining and warm company. The sun had now set, and the fairy lights and candles sprinkled throughout the roof deck were all lit, lending an atmosphere of fireside chat, a perfect setting for Antonio's revelations.

CHAPTER 36

The conversation naturally led to our wedding and the reception.

"Carli, you outdid yourself my friend," said Amy, her voice filled with genuine admiration. Her words resonated in the air, emphasizing the effort that had gone into the celebration.

I smiled, grateful for her kind words, but felt compelled to remind everyone of the true contributors to that day's success.

"Our *mamás* deserve all the credit, you know that. All I did, all we did," I said, glancing at my husband, "was get ourselves ready and show up at all the events, including the day of. That's it." Manuel nodded in agreement.

"You took care of your dress, and it's the most amazing wedding dress I *ever* saw!" Said Luna, always loyal, always giving me credit for things.

Her words caused a blush to rise to my cheeks, the gentle warmth spreading across my face.

"No small feat on that, I gotta say! It *was* just gorgeous, gorgeous, gorgeous, Carli. If I got myself hitched again, I sure would want a dress just like it!" Said Amy, excitement evident in her voice.

"Hey. Wife! You're not getting yourself hitched unless it's to me again. *¿Entiende usted?*" Douglas, smiling, asserted in bad Spanish, encircling Amy with his arm, and she sank into his side, their love palpable. Do you understand.

His comment evoked another round of laughter, the mirth resonating all around. We all clinked glasses.

In seconds, the inviting scents of chocolate and chilis from Manuel's chicken *mole* reached us as Umberto placed a large shallow bowl of it on the table.

After appetizers, we'd all stood to admire the view with the lights coming on all around town in the distant hills, as well as the lights on the spires of the church, but now the delicious smell beckoned us back to our seats.

"What a feast, Manuel, wow, wow, wow!" Said Amy, spreading her arms wide as if we couldn't see the food for ourselves.

After Antonio was done eating, he poured himself a half glass of wine, sat back from the table like a king settling into his throne, which told me he was about to start.

The rest of us, finished or not, put our forks down. Our favorite detective sergeant tended to eat faster than anyone else.

Without preamble, he got to what we all wanted to hear. "Well, strangely, on the morning of the day before the wedding of these two," he said, extending his arms outwards in a grand gesture, as if spotlighting Manuel and me at opposite ends of the table, drawing everyone's attention to our presence, as though they didn't already know we were there.

"I received an envelope with some information about that skeleton in Eduardo Caldero's garden," he revealed.

His voice resonated in the night air. After he said it, he waited long enough so that his words hung heavy, like the air before a storm. His intense gaze fixed on me while he spoke, the dark pools of his eyes unblinking.

"No way!" Said Douglas and Amy almost at the same time. Amy, who knew about my past investigations into killings, glanced my way.

"Yeah, no way!" Luna exclaimed, pretending. I shot her a meaningful glance, the kind that meant for her to keep silent. She winked at me discreetly.

Antonio turned to her, his lips curling into a wry smile, knowing full well that Luna knew, that I told her most everything. This confirmed for me that Antonio was certain of my role in all this. During the next few days, he would insist that I tell him everything I'd done in my investigations, but not now.

Manuel, for his part, just looked down at his plate, his gaze lost in the remnants of the chicken mole. He discreetly gave me a languid blink, sending me comfort from across the table, grounding me amidst the swirling emotions that overcame me, all the dangerous things that had happened during my investigation—I had fought a man, even!

· • ● ● ● · ● ● ● • ·

I'd recounted the whole story to Manuel during an afternoon at the vineyard. We had strolled between the rows of grapevines basking in the warm sun. A soft breeze had carried the rich scents of ripe grapes and the soil beneath our feet, which had served well as a backdrop to our murmured conversation.

To my surprise, he wasn't angry with me. He calmly explained that as my husband, he felt it was his duty to look after me, his partner in life, and hoped I felt the same about him. He understood my desire to solve crimes affecting our community, friends, and family.

He admitted that he sometimes felt a similar urge but prioritized our safety, the life we were building, and our future together, including our children, the success of Manuel's Eatery, Carli's Secret Closet, and the *hacienda*.

He chose to let go of these impulses, trusting Antonio, an experienced and competent detective, to handle these mysteries. He acknowledged that Antonio's heavy workload might slow down the investigations, but he had confidence in his abilities.

It brought tears to my eyes to hear him say how important our life together was to him, a proclamation more potent than the sweetest grapes growing all around us. His words brushed against my heart, leaving an imprint.

In the end, he'd made me promise that if I felt the urge to involve myself in police business, to break my promise, that I'd share my concerns with him. Together, we'd figure out what to do.

• • • ● •● ● • • •

Now, all of us at the table leaned in toward Antonio, and waited with our breaths held for him to continue, the murmur of anticipation a tangible presence.

He cleared his throat and continued. The melody of background music from one of my Spotify playlists filled the air around us, resonating from the speakers scattered across the rooftop. I grabbed my phone and turned down the volume so we could hear Antonio better.

"So, first, Eduardo didn't kill anyone, in case any of you wonder about that." He said, his words clear in the nighttime air.

"Oh, that's good to know," I couldn't help saying, an involuntary smirk playing on my lips.

He gave me such a piercing look, a glacier in his gaze, that I had to look away, feeling a pang of guilt about getting myself involved in what was, admittedly, his business. And not mine.

"So, good for Eduardo who I don't know, but if he's not the one who put a body in his own garden, who did? Like, who is he, first of all?" Asked Amy, eyebrows knitted together in sincere curiosity.

To keep Antonio talking about the arrests and what happened, I briefed her on who Eduardo was and his connection to Sofia whom Amy knew.

"Oh, gotcha," she responded, comprehension lighting up her face.

Antonio went on with his story.

"Eduardo, right now, he's under *arresto domiciliario*." House arrest.

"Oh, that's good," I couldn't help but interject, despite the wave of concern and images of confinement this brought up in my mind. But it was better than being in jail. The very idea made my stomach turn on Eduardo's behalf.

Antonio ignored me, and continued, his voice steady and strong, probably tired by now of being interrupted while doing his favorite thing: telling us all about how *he'd* solved the crimes he'd solved.

"When someone buries a dead person without calling us, it's a crime of *ocultamiento de un cadáver*." Concealment of a corpse.

Amy opened her mouth to say something, but Antonio put up a hand like a stop sign, a quiet order that hung in the air.

Instead, she picked up her wine glass and took a sip, her eyes big on Antonio, while Douglas kept a thoughtful, borderline contemplative gaze on my cousin.

"Eduardo can be punished by imprisonment and fines, but considering his clean track record until now and this being an accident, he might continue to just be held at home, and he might have to pay a fine." He stopped talking to take a sip of wine, the glass making a muted clinking sound against his teeth.

Douglas seized the brief opportunity to ask a question. "How long will he have to be on house arrest? And how much is the fine for something like that?" His eyes showed a deep curiosity. Douglas, a businessman, seemed to find this fascinating and exciting despite the dark side of it all.

"That depends on the judge. But it's from a few months up to several years. In Eduardo's case, I think it will just be months," Antonio speculated, an uncharacteristic uncertainty seeping into his voice. "He didn't plan it, that's clear by the journal pages that were verified to have been written years back, and him having no reason at all to kill his cousin. But it's up to the judge, not me."

"Well, I hope it turns out okay for him. He's well-loved in his family, and in the community," I interjected. "And I've always liked him," as if that would matter, which of course, it did not.

"Good, but again, we don't know what a judge will think. We'll see. I'm just happy it's figured out, one less thing for me to do." He sighed, the weariness obvious in the gravelly cadence of his voice. He groaned and stretched, the back of his chair creaking with his movements.

This display of fatigue made me yawn, which I managed to suppress, but Manuel caught it from across the table. His eyes crinkled in gentle amusement as he blew me a kiss, which I returned with a soft smile. Our marital activities must be tiring me out. The thought made me blush, but I forced my mind back to Antonio.

"In the end, the family reported their Alberto to the police just for the sake of saying they did something, but we did not do much about it. I read the report. Police went to his home and found no sign of foul play. He was a grown man, in the *cartel*, and so many go missing ..." he trailed off.

A thick silence followed, heavy with the knowledge that the police hadn't done much to find a missing man, and with the unspoken reality of *cartel* violence.

Luna broke the spell, her voice a welcomed ripple in the stillness.

"But why would he have a gardener dig a hole where he buried him?" She asked, her tone full of disbelief.

"Oh, well. This is the interesting part," Antonio declared, a spark of enthusiasm lighting his voice. "The skeleton would not have been found if Eduardo's wife had not nagged him for more than a year about planting an orange tree in their back-yard," he continued, his tone turning a bit theatrical, which underlined the astonishing turn of events even more.

"When Eduardo finally agreed, he called Ramon Gonzalez's company to do it. The problem came when the supervisor told the two gardeners who he sent to do the job to plant it on the right side when looking at the house from the back of the property, and nearer to the back wall than to the house."

He'd moved on to coffee, and stopped to take a sip, a mis-chievous smile playing on his lips. He loved that we were all hanging on to his words. I rolled my eyes.

"Antonio!" I exclaimed. Luna and Amy let out a laugh at my impatience.

"Mi amor ...," said my new husband, no doubt wanting me to give Antonio the space and the time he needed.

A few drops of rain fell on us. We waited, unsure whether to seek shelter from an impending shower.

After a full minute, Antonio, as if he'd been bestowed special powers by the rain gods, declared that there would be no more, so we could stay on my roof.

The air carried a fresh scent, infused with the earthy scent of recent rainfall, which meant it had rained harder nearby.

"Okay, my favorite cousin, go on." I decided to let him tell us everything in his own way because otherwise, he might stop talking all together even if he loved doing it. You never knew with Antonio.

He went on, but about the wrong subject. "Oh, I'm your favorite now?" He asked, a smile dancing in his eyes and curling at the corners of his mouth.

"I guess that *vato* is your husband now. Okay."

Everyone laughed, me included.

Finally, we got the rest of the story. "So, you see, Eduardo says he told the supervisor to plant the new tree on the right side of the yard, when looking at it from the *back door* of the house, not from the back wall."

I sucked in my breath and so did Luna. We stared at one another. What a piece of bad luck for Eduardo! Imagining the flood of thoughts and emotions that must have surged through his mind when he first saw that the gardener had uncovered the skeleton. It sent a shiver down my spine.

The scene unfolded in my mind's eye as Antonio explained what happened. I could see the gardeners, their hands covered in soil, diligently digging the hole to plant the tree, their movements precise and determined. And then, the resonant thud of the shovel striking bone. I shivered at the thought.

Amy and Douglas looked at one another, then turned their gaze to the rest of us.

"That's it? He got caught because a gardener didn't follow instructions?" Astonishment creased Amy's face, while Douglas's features contorted with a quizzical expression.

"No, no," said Antonio, his voice holding a tinge of resignation, like a soft sigh. "It's because the supervisor gave the gardener the wrong instructions. That's all it takes sometimes to catch a criminal. Someone else messing up somewhere along the line.

"And you know the rest. The gardeners called us." His voice betrayed his resignation over how such things happened sometimes.

"That's so, so sad ..." said Amy. Douglas put his arm around her shoulders and squeezed. Then, she sat straighter suddenly, looking like she'd just remembered something important. "And wait, speaking of Ramon Gonzalez's company, how did he die?"

Antonio looked at me, looking surprised. Clearly, he'd assumed I'd passed the news around after he'd let me know.

I shifted in my chair. "Oh, Amy, I'm so sorry, what with everything going on ... I meant to call and let you know that it was a heart attack."

"Ah ... well, at least it wasn't another murder." She turned to Douglas and planted a kiss on his cheek.

Looking at her, I decided she'd probably had a thought that the same could happen to her husband.

From the roofs of a few neighboring houses, several dogs barked all at once, signaling that someone they didn't know was nearby, but a wave of relief washed over me as I realized that The Followers wouldn't be trying to get into my house again, thank goodness. Plus, with my *husband* here, I'd like to see their faces when faced with the ferociousness of Manuel when the situation called for it.

Luna and I exchanged a sad look over Eduardo's unfortunate situation.

However, that fleeting exchange transformed into a silent understanding between us, a mutual agreement to encourage

Antonio to move forward and tell us about the arrests regarding Aurelia's murder, the thing we both most yearned to know.

Using only our eyes, I conveyed to Luna that she should take the initiative and speak up. Otherwise, we could be up until dawn waiting for Antonio to finish the story.

CHAPTER 37

Luna, her dark eyes flashing with a mix of curiosity and caution, turned to Antonio.

"So, *vato*, what about the Gonzalezes? What happened there?"

"Well, now that was a bit more complicated to solve," he said, a flicker of pride on his face. He straightened his posture, his chest swelling with bravado.

Suppressing an eyeroll, my fingers closed around the stem of my wine glass, and I decided to take a sip of wine instead of responding. But then, I couldn't help it.

"You had help, though, right?" I asked.

The air hung heavy much like just before a big storm. Manuel's gaze met mine from across the table, urging me to stay silent.

Instead of ignoring me, Antonio decided to address it. "Yes, Carli. A *lot* of help, actually," he said, his voice laced with a bit of anger and frustration. "One day ..." He grumbled, playing with his teaspoon.

All of us went on alert. Maybe Antonio would go on a rampage now? Why, oh why, had I said that?

"Carli is going to get herself in trouble one of these days. I'm goin ... hey!" Antonio's words were cut short, a sudden yelp escaping him.

Manuel's eyes bore into our cousin, a different kind of storm brewing in there. I suspected he had discreetly kicked Antonio under the table for his disrespectful tone. I sat up straighter, feeling the electricity in the air. My man had my back ...

Everyone else remained silent, sensing the machismo flowing between them like colliding forces of nature, quiet spectators to the clash of the two men's egos.

"Just tell us the rest, Antonio, *vato*. It's getting late. *Por favor*. And I think we all know that Carli managed to get some information to you. Information that helped."

Manuel whispered, but no one could miss the command in his words.

I held my breath as Antonio and my husband locked eyes, a silent battle of wills continuing to play out before us. After a tense moment, Antonio nodded, followed by Manuel.

Out of respect for them both, I managed to suppress the smirk building up at the corners of my mouth.

Antonio continued. "We made many arrests. Two days after the wedding." The crisp authority in his tone cut through the tension in our group, capturing our attention.

As his words hung there, the bells of a distant church began pealing, lending somberness to the moment.

As soon as the tolling stopped, its final echoes fading away, Antonio resumed talking, his words carving through our silence.

He rearranged himself in his chair, and took another sip of coffee.

"We learned through an informer that Santiago Ortega, Pablo Ortega's brother, was hiding out in a smaller hotel up San Francisco street."

"Ooh, an informer," said Luna. I gave her a look to remain quiet. I wanted to hear this.

"I had eight officers with me, and we covered the front and had three of them on the roof before we went to his room. In case he decided that would be a way to escape." He shrugged, as if to say it was procedure.

Manuel nodded, obviously in agreement with the tactic. The rest of us held a rapt silence, everyone captivated by what Antonio was now saying.

"So, we knocked at his door and identified ourselves. And no response, and no one in the room. What we didn't know," he chuckled, "is that the manager was a friend of his, and he texted Santiago as soon as we asked for his room number."

Other than Manuel, who'd experienced similar situations in his years as a detective, we were all riveted to Antonio even more.

"But with officers inside the door of the hotel and on the roof, they didn't have much of a way to escape."

Amy couldn't help but interject here.

"What do you mean, they?" She asked, having moved forward in her chair.

"Well, it turned out that two other men, the ones that had been following, you, Carli," he looked in my direction, "were with him. So, it was three of them trying to leave." He shook his head, his expression showing bemusement at their foolish attempt to escape from him and his team.

"What we didn't know yet, is that this hotel is connected to another small hotel next door, and that, through the service corridor, you can get to that other hotel. Same owners, using the same staff for both hotels."

"No way!" Exclaimed Luna, glancing at me. "So, they got away. But, I thought you said you caught them!"

"If you'll let me finish," said Antonio, giving her a look and clearing his throat.

"When all three of them exited from the hotel next door, my officers who'd been outside the hotel saw them and alerted us all."

"By the time me and the rest of my guys got outside, three officers were chasing Santiago and his cronies down the street toward the Jardin. So, of course, we ran after them." He worried his mouth, as if thinking of what to say next.

"My guys jumped them just before we got there but those idiots thought they could fight eight cops, so, it took some doing to get them cuffed. They kept punching and kicking, and swearing, and one even spit in an officer's face. That caballero got a good kick in the you-know-whats for doing that."

There were a few winces around the table, us imagining what that must have felt like.

He continued. "So, we had get them cuffed, right, but then a car pulled up fast and slammed on the brakes, like they were stopping at a pit stop on a racetrack. And four scruffy looking guys came out of it. With guns drawn, believe it or not." He laughed at this.

"What ... wait ... why would they pull out guns in front of the police? That's just crazy," I said, my mouth dropping open, thinking that I'd started all that with my sleuthing. Antonio could have been killed!

"These *vatos* are just crazy, Carli. They don't think more than two minutes ahead," said Antonio.

I turned to Manuel who was nodding his agreement. Everyone else stared at Antonio, still fascinated by his account of the arrest.

"One got off a shot, but one of my guys tackled him at the same time, and the bullet went off into the air, and ..." He trailed off to pour himself more coffee.

"*¿En serio?* Antonio ..." this from Luna, who like me, often got impatient with how Antonio liked to dramatize accounts of his police work, and stop talking at crucial moments in the story.

Manuel glanced at her and chuckled. Amy and Douglas said not a word, instead still hanging on to every one of Antonio's words, their hands gripped together.

Car horns went off down the street, someone shouted. We waited to hear if anything more would come of that, then Antonio went on with the story.

"We were lucky that the bullet came back down a ways from us. It took out a good chunk out of a cobblestone, then stayed right there. It could have ricocheted and hit one of us," he said, gazing around at us all to see if we understood that he himself could have been hurt.

We did, but since he survived—which we knew since he was right here—we were all more interested in knowing what happened next.

"That *maleante* is lucky he didn't get killed, that one of my guys didn't shoot him." He shook his head in disbelief at the man's action. Wrongdoer.

"Those four had to be disarmed and cuffed, too." Antonio seemed to go into a reverie then, recalling the event.

"So, seven arrests all at the same time! It was late when I left the station that night," he chuckled.

"I can't believe this happened just next to the Jardin. Is it not safe anywhere anymore?" Asked Amy, looking distressed.

"This almost never happens. I can't recall a shooting or cartel fights near the Jardin. It never happened when I was on the force, but ..." said Manuel, lifting his eyes and chin to Antonio.

"He's right. But, the cartels have been moving in here, trying to extort money from local businesses, and selling drugs." He looked off into the distance.

Not a word was said about that by any of us, everyone contemplating what it could mean for the future of the town we all loved.

"But, we have a huge presence in Centro, as you know. So, the criminals try to stay away from there as much as possible."

"Who were those guys, the shooters?" Asked Douglas.

"Cartelista. There to try and keep us from arresting Santiago Ortega and his sidekicks. It turned out they hadn't even been ordered to do it. They were high on drugs and made the decision themselves. They'll now sit out a lot of years behind bars." Cartel members.

"So, they were *all cartel*?" This from Luna.

"Sí." Antonio gazed at her, sensing her distress. We were all troubled by the increase in crime due to cartel activity. But we couldn't live in fear every day.

We were all hanging on his words, our bodies leaning in his direction, but Dap chose this moment to come twirl himself around my legs, meowing like he felt left out. From the other side of the table, Manuel clucked and extended his hand to him, and Dap, the traitor, made his way to him instead.

My husband scooped him up, his touch gentle and reassuring, and produced a treat from his pocket.

Would Dap now become Manuel's cat instead of mine? I couldn't help but wonder.

"Manuel, *mi amor*, he'll get fat," I said.

"No, Dapper, *vato*. You won't get fat, *sí*? Don't get me into trouble with your *mamá*, okay?" he said, pretending to share a secret with Dap. "Just go up and down the stairs a couple more times each day, and I'll keep spoiling you with treats. *¿Entender?*" You understand. He concluded with a nod, emphasizing his point.

I struggled to maintain my feigned annoyance at the situation. But how could I stay upset with my *guapo* husband? Watching him, a strong, handsome man being so gentle with the small creature that was Dap, softened my resolve, and a smile tugged at the corners of my lips.

"You two and that cat ..." Said Antonio, his voice laced with amusement.

Amy and Luna burst into laughter, while Douglas smiled, his eyes twinkling with warmth. Manuel and I gazed at one another, love shining from his eyes, and surely from mine.

The episode lightened the mood considerably, and that might well have been Dap's intent.

Finally, our Antonio took another sip of coffee and continued the story.

"We worked those guys. Quite a bit." He glanced at Manuel here, looking as if he were saying something without speaking.

Manuel, his chin on his hand now, raised his eyebrows in understanding at his friend, his ex-colleague.

I noticed, of course, and asked. "What?"

My husband and my cousin glanced at one another, a silent understanding that they weren't going to answer that. I gave Manuel my best dirty look, and then transferred it to Antonio. Manuel put a finger across his mouth vertically so that I'd drop the subject. His eyes told me that he'd explain later. I guessed that Antonio didn't want to discuss police tactics while in good company.

"It took four days of questioning, but one of the men who'd been with Santiago, he cracked, finally."

"I knew it was him!!" I exclaimed, my voice escalating to yell, excitement getting the better of me.

Antonio turned in my direction. "Him who? I didn't say who did it yet." He frowned at me.

I shrugged at him and tsk'd, annoyed.

"So, before I got the killer to admit everything, we had police in Mexico City go to his house. And guess what we found there?" He wore a look of self-satisfaction on his face, and gave us all his best imitation of a Chesire cat smile.

No one replied, so he continued, but in a gentler tone of voice. "Aurelia's engagement and wedding rings ..." he trailed off.

I sucked in a breath, and so did the others, except for Manuel, who'd likely heard worse. Firecrackers went off, which got the roof dogs to bark, so for a moment, it was too loud and distracting for anyone to talk.

As soon as the chaos calmed, I asked. "But, which one, whose house, Antonio? Which one of them was the killer?" I leaned toward him, and so did the others, even Manuel.

He milked the moment some more, but then got on with the story. "Well, they were all in cahoots, it turns out," he said, looking my way. I already knew that because of the conversation I'd overheard in that shop. I wanted to know who had suffocated Aurelia!

"Antonio ..." I said, now impatient. Luna looked annoyed, too, sitting straighter in her chair, looking pointedly at my cousin. Manuel lounged, giving that same cousin an irritated look. Douglas and Amy just sat, hand in hand, faces immobile, not saying a thing, which was telling. Antonio was getting on all our nerves.

"So, what I did was this. I told each of them that the others had ratted him out. That he should make a deal before the others did, so that things turned out better for him." He stretched his neck in all directions.

"It took a while as I said, but finally, the first one cracked. And he gave up his '*amigos*' without any remorse that I could see."

Then, he went silent.

"*Who*?" I asked, exasperated.

He smirked at me before telling us what we'd all been waiting to hear.

"Santiago Ortega did the deed." He murmured it, then gazed down at the table, possibly recalling the interrogation and what it had taken to get the men to confess.

Everyone around the table let out their own form of exclamation.

Me? I took credit for my hard work. "I knew it, I knew it, I knew it," I said.

This offended my detective sergeant cousin. "No, you didn't. Otherwise, you would have told me, and you wouldn't have been sitting here all evening, waiting for *me* to tell *you*!"

"Well, I gave you all of them on a silver platter, as they say. You wouldn't have known about them without me. And he was one of them." I sat back in my chair and crossed my arms, pouting.

Antonio opened his mouth ready with a retort, but Manuel spoke up. "*Niños*. No fighting. Please." Children.

Antonio and I, both fuming, glanced at him, then back at one another, and concurred to move on with a nod.

"We suspected him most actually, because we found the rings at his house."

I exhaled, and my eyes stung, thinking of Aurelia wearing her beautiful rings.

"Once that happened, we leaned into Mr. Ortega. Hard." He looked around the table, at each of us, telling us without saying it that there might have been some physical convincing going on, too ...

It made me uncomfortable that Antonio might have resorted to that to extract the truth from Santiago.

I caught a look from Manuel that said I should let it go. I'm sure he could see my annoyance over him trying to get me to do something his way, the third time tonight. But I also realized that it wasn't up to me how Antonio did his policing.

And also, that the man was a killer! He'd killed my friend, my neighbor! Looking at it like that, Antonio could tell him any lie he wanted to get him to confess.

"In any case, we also told him that if he confessed, things would go easier for him. That it might lead to a reduced sentence or a plea bargain, or something else to make his time in prison easier, or shorter."

"Is that true?" Amy's voice quivered with uncertainty.

Antonio's gaze bore into her, his eyes narrowing with irritation at her questioning of his expertise in such matters, and at the naivete of her inquiry, but he didn't answer her question.

Luna interrupted this small drama by asking her own compromising question.

"Even though he *killed* someone?" Luna's voice oozed shock, her own disbelief evident.

Antonio's eyes flicked toward her then, but he went on with his story without answering her either.

"It took him a while to break down and tell us the truth of it, but in the end, he did," he said, his voice laced with satisfaction, raising his eyebrows and chin in Manuel's direction. The flickering candle on the table danced on my love's face, which remained passive, his eyes a cool veil, betraying none of his thoughts on the matter.

A dull throb pulsed in my chest, my heart aching for my husband, who had once been involved in this kind of dark and dangerous work. Trading his gun for a chef's knife had been a good move. It suited him, and us. Yet, in his distant gaze during Antonio's crime tales, I sensed a lingering hunger for the thrill of the chase. Across the table, I sent him a soft kiss, a silent echo of my enduring love and support.

For Antonio, doing this kind of work was a calling, I knew, a sense of purpose that went deep as his bones, an innate part of his being that radiated from him.

"So, go on," said Amy, anticipation flattening her lips into a thin line, as if holding herself back from asking questions, so anxious was she to hear the rest of the story.

It made me smile.

Antonio obliged her. "Well, *Mr.* Contreras decided to kill Aurelia Gonzalez ... on the spur of the moment. He said it was just a crazy thought he had ..."

The words tumbled from his lips, each one laden with a profound sense of regret, like stones dropping into a still pond.

He paused, letting the full weight of what he'd just said sink in.

CHAPTER 38

T hat revelation hit us all like a bolt of lightning, the air charged with disbelief.

Amy's eyes widened, and her hand flew to her mouth, attempting to stifle the gasp that escaped her.

Luna sat on the edge of her chair; her body stiffened with shock. From the corner of my eye, I could see her mouth had dropped open.

Douglas's brows furrowed deeper with each passing moment, casting shadows over his eyes as he stared at Antonio, while Manuel's gaze flickered in my direction, watching for my reaction.

All this I saw in fleeting glances. Antonio's revelation shocked me and my gaze, clouded by impending tears, found him again.

My friend, my mother's friend, a good woman liked and loved by many, had died because of a madman's *whim*?

Antonio, after the bomb he'd dropped on us, looked lost in a haunting reverie, and it took him a moment before he could go on.

"He did it because he wanted to save his twin from punishment for not paying back his debt." His voice resonated across the deck, his solemn pronouncement blending with the hum of San Miguel at night, life going on as usual below our rooftop gathering.

His complexion had turned the red of deep anger, something he most likely had to work hard to control in his work. No matter how angry he'd ever been with me, he'd never looked this red.

"That's pretty bad!" exclaimed Amy, anger in her own voice. She'd said out loud what all of us were thinking. In the glow of the candles dispersed around the deck and of the fairy lights strung above us across the rooftop, I could see the wetness in her eyes.

Douglas patted her hand, offering a comforting touch amidst her rising emotions.

A distant siren sounded, its shrill whine adding to the tension of the others in addition to mine—an invisible electric current crackling all around us, a static charge of collective sorrow and grief.

I nodded at Amy, in agreement with her statement. My eyes welled up even more, turning the flames of the candles into blurry orbs, as the weight of the tragedy pressed upon my heart. I blinked away the tears, determined to focus on Antonio's words.

To think that Aurelia had died because of such tragically flawed decision making!

From out of nowhere, a strange thought came to me. Could it be that, in some perverse, twisted way, this senseless act had spared Aurelia from a life of unbearable grief?

She and Ramon had shared an unbreakable bond, and the notion of her living without him seemed as impossible as waking up to a day where the sun didn't rise.

I dismissed those confusing thoughts. Aurelia had had so much to live for, even without Ramon by her side. Her love for her two daughters, her son, her three grandchildren, and the prospect of more to come was as undeniable as the barking roof dogs of San Miguel, of the churches' bells erupting at all hours, as ... as ... my love for Manuel and his for me.

Aurelia had had a vibrant life, participating in the Música Clásica Esencial group and engaging in various charitable endeavors. She'd had a multitude of friends, one of whom was my own *mamá*. The thought of explaining this to her chilled me more than the cool evening breeze.

Because she knew what Antonio had come to do tonight, she was sure to ask us about it tomorrow at Sunday *comida*, her inquiry now a looming specter under the night sky. I shivered for reasons that had nothing to do with the breeze.

"Yes, it's pretty bad," said Antonio. His resigned tone was the somber serenade of someone who'd heard too many such stories.

"He decided to do it when he heard about Ramon Gonzalez having died because he thought that, then, Pablo's wife would have her inheritance right away and could pay Pablo's gambling debt to the *cartel*. His brother would be saved."

He shrugged his shoulders, head swaying from side to side, as though dancing to a silent rhythm only he could hear.

"Maybe it's true what they say that twins will do more for each other than for other siblings," I mused.

Antonio looked at me skeptically, while in the dim light, Luna and Amy nodded in agreement, their movements subtle.

Manuel and Douglas remained silent; their thoughts hidden behind stoic expressions.

I left that thought on the table, so that Antonio could tell us the rest without stretching his story until dawn, something he'd find easy to do.

"So, Antonio. What happened after?" I asked, my curiosity cutting through the weight of his revelation.

"Nothing. He confessed, he's in jail. *And* ... his lawyer, he's a high-powered one. From Mexico City." The words tumbled from his mouth.

We all stared at him, wondering why the emphasis on the fact he had a lawyer from Mexico City. I noticed Manuel's grim and knowing expression, which told me that he knew what that meant. The dim light created by the candles and fairy lights threw stark shadows across his face, making his look even more intense.

"What?" I asked, my eyes darting back and forth between them, feeling confused.

Antonio nodded in Manuel's direction, signaling him to answer.

"It means a *cartel* lawyer, Carlita," Manuel said in a near whisper, his words hanging heavy over our group.

"It means he's getting help from his *jefe* with the attorney fees. It means he's a valuable member of the organization, despite this mess he created here."

He cleared his throat and took a sip of his coffee. I remained silent, stunned by the fact that a *cartel* had killed my friend, my neighbor, my customer.

"That's just crazy, all this stuff happening here." Said Luna, her words like whispers through the night air.

Each of us agreed with her in one way or another, all of us silent, lost in thought.

Antonio pulled us out of our reveries. "So, that's it. It's all over until the trial starts. The Gonzalez family can grieve in peace, knowing the killer was caught and will pay for what he did. At least, their consolation is that their parents are together forever."

Now, we knew it all. Except for one thing.

"Wait, Antonio. What about those two men? What happened to them?"

"The ones following you?" He asked, his tongue planted firmly in cheek, a hesitant playful note in his voice.

Who else could I mean?

"Yes, them, duh," I replied, tired, and now annoyed with his verbal theatrics.

"Nothing happened. We questioned them and had to let them go. Nothing to hold them with after Santiago confessed. They did nothing that I could arrest them on. Them following you wouldn't last long if we charged them with that."

"Oh?" I wondered out loud, glancing at Manuel.

"Well, Carli, their lawyer would be sure to come up with all sorts of good reasons as to why you kept running into them, and the fight you had with the one? Well, it's his word against yours. You don't have witnesses. It would be too hard to prove, Carli."

He spoke softly, a whisper carrying a hard truth, knowing full well I found it offensive that the word of someone like him would have equal value to mine in a court of law.

My cheeks blazed like our city skyline at sunset, the heat of my anger rising to my face.

"That is ... that's, urgh, I *hate* that!"

The murmuring consolations of my friends and my husband swirled around me, their words only background noise to my fast-beating heart.

Manuel, sensing my distress, came to me. He brought his chair next to mine, then sat and took my hand in both of his with a tenderness that comforted me.

I yearned to vent my indignation even more, but as I opened my mouth to do so, Umberto and Maria re-emerged onto the rooftop. They busied themselves clearing our dirty dinner plates and near-empty platters from the side table.

Manuel gave my hand a reassuring squeeze, then gave me a look that I instantly recognized. He didn't want to share such information with his staff who would undoubtedly gossip about their *jefe*'s wife having fought a man, one from a *cartel*, no less!

Seizing the moment, I decided to propose a toast. I winked at Manuel and rose, wine glass in hand. Tapping it twice with a random spoon lying on the table, I drew attention to myself and began.

"Well, we can all rest easy now that all this mayhem is over. The bad guys are in custody and can't hurt any of us anymore. Thank you to my favorite cousin for all his hard work in protecting us."

Raising my glass toward Antonio, I toasted him. Luna quickly followed suit, lifting her own glass toward him, and the others chimed in.

Antonio blushed like I'd never seen him do before. Despite his posturing, deep down, he felt humble about the whole thing, I could tell.

Before we could all reseat ourselves, Antonio rose to his feet and raised his coffee cup in my direction, and said, "To you, Carli ... thank you."

My turn to blush.

For some inexplicable reason, perhaps to relieve the tension we'd all felt over the past hour, laughter bubbled up amongst us. As it echoed across the rooftop, we sat back down and fell into a comfortable rhythm of small talk, straying away from anything remotely criminal.

After a while, Amy returned us to the subject by saying, "Hey, y'all, no more solving murders when I'm outta town! I'm in on the next one!"

Manuel and I turned to each other, eyes locked, and said in loud voices, "There is no next one!" in unison, as if we'd rehearsed it.

Our harmonized denial sparked laughter from Amy. I ignored the small niggling feeling somewhere deep inside me, because, of course, there could be no more murders for me to get involved in. I was married, and with luck, would become a mother in a not too-distant future.

Yes, echoed a voice in my head. No more of this mayhem disrupting my life, no matter how exhilarating it was to solve such mysteries. The danger was too great, not just for me, but for my family.

So, once again, yes, *todo está bien con mi mundo*, I thought. All is well with my world.

Dared I hope that this time, it *would* be forever?

Carli wants for everything to remain well in her world, sure. But, you know, life (and mayhem) happens ...

Cozy up with more Carli Cano mysteries—Just two quick clicks, and voilà – you're diving into your next amazing read at your favorite online bookstore!

When Music Meets Murder (Book 1)

When Mayhem Means Murder (Book 2)

Mayhem No More (Book 3)

Stitched in Deceit (The Prequel That Started It All!)

Got a print copy and eager to find all the links to the next books in one handy spot? Just head over to Carli's corner on my website – you'll find everything you need right there!

https://maryselaflamme.com/carli-cano-mystery-series

LOVED THE BOOK? PLEASE BE A HERO IN MY STORY!

I f you had fun with Carli and crew, the best way to support my work is by leaving a quick review!

Seriously—reviews are rocket fuel for indie authors like me. We don't survive without them.

I don't have the big bucks needed to plaster Times Square with ads, but I *can* reach more readers with your help.
Just a few words—no sonnets required (though I'd totally frame one if you wrote it).

Here's the direct link to leave your review:
https://maryselaflamme.com/review/

Your words help more than you know—and keeps future books coming.

Thank you from me, Carli, Manuel, Antonio, Luna ... and the rest of the fictional gang. You really are the cherry on top.

The Author

Meet **Maryse Laflamme**—the *matcha-sipping, mystery-spinning, bone-broth-brewing badass* who turned a death sentence into a launchpad. At 71, she's living proof that reinvention has no age limit—from crafting compelling fiction in whatever corner of the world the wind last tossed her, to building an author empire powered by no-bloat blueprints and digital smarts.

She writes like she's talking to her sharpest, sassiest friend—and helps writers skip the overwhelm and actually finish their damn books. When she's not spinning worldly mysteries with grit, glamour, and just enough danger to keep you up at night, she's probably baking bread. Or taking a hike. Her voice? Irreverent, insightful, and infused with wisdom earned from a life well-traveled—and almost lost.

She made an incurable cancer her bitch, and came back armed with a pen, a plan, a story to tell, a vision to share, and zero patience for small talk or safe choices. And sometimes? She goes radio silent for no reason. Don't ask...

Wanna take a look into Maryse Laflamme's World?

Got questions, comments, or your own mini-mystery to share? Reach out through the contact form on her website. She's a reply wizard, unless you're sending Spam—then expect to be catapulted to the farthest reaches of the Universe!

Stalk—uh, no, *follow* her online!

Here's where you can catch her occasional musings and clues:

Website: MaryseLaflamme.com

Facebook: Maryse Laflamme Writer

Instagram: @maryselaflammewriter

www.ingramcontent.com/pod-product-compliance
Lightning Source LLC
Chambersburg PA
CBHW030655260626
47157CB00007B/2664